WRONG PLACE, WRIGHT TIME

Wrong, Wright, book 3

MEGAN WADE

Copyright © 2021 by Megan Wade

All rights reserved.

No part of this book may be reproduced in any form or by any electronic or mechanical means, including information storage and retrieval systems, without written permission from the author, except for the use of brief quotations in a book review.

❦ Created with Vellum

ISLA

Swiping a layer of plum-colored lipstick over my mouth, I take a moment to assess my appearance in the bathroom mirror, wondering if my outfit is too plain or demure for where I'm going, which is a drag show in Midtown East. I've never been to one before, but I imagine wearing a pencil skirt and a cap sleeve blouse is a little too... board meeting for something that sounds so colorful and exciting.

With a side-to-side turn, I run my hand along the hem of the lilac silk on my blouse while I contemplate whether I want to tuck it into my skirt. There's a drag queen in Australia who goes by the moniker, *Karen from Finance*. She's hilarious and fun, and her entire demeanor seems to light up a room despite the corporate theme of her character. If I were a drag queen, my name would be *Isla from PR*, and I'd be decidedly unfun since all I ever do in life is work, work, work then moan about needing to work so I can avoid going out to have fun.

I think my social skills are broken.

And it's no wonder. It's been so long since I've been on a date or done anything for the sake of enjoyment that I think I've forgotten how.

As one of the handful of children set to inherit the *Write Media Corporation* when our parents retire, I'm expected to pull long hours at work learning every facet of running a company with interests the size of ours. My father and two uncles currently sit at the helm, and together they control the vast majority of information that the American people get fed each morning. We don't own all media, of course, there are plenty of alternative sources out there and other media groups who hold the rights to different channels, but we have enough of a monopoly that our reach is far and extensive.

That monopoly also means that the interests of many are governed by a bunch of old men who are so far out of touch with the current climate, that the only girl child in the family who works for the company can't stand to work even remotely close to them. I tried when I first finished college, but after months of sitting around the boardroom table being talked over and asked to top up coffees was enough for me.

So to save my sanity while also keeping my

paycheck, I've sequestered myself a few floors down in the Public Relations department, because at least then I'm seen to be taking on an active role instead of just sitting in a massive corner office using my surname like a powerful sword to get my way.

You know, it's amazing what a well-timed, insinuating article can do to not only influence the public, but politicians too. It all feels a little bit dirty to me most days. But I do enjoy the money that comes with my station. I'm not going to lie about that. And when I finally get the chance to take over when my father retires, I get my chance to make some up-to-date changes to the way we do things. But until then, I keep my head down and my mouth shut. Especially since my big brother, Ash, was completely cut off for not falling in line—he chose to be an engineer instead of a junior VP.

Both Ash and our cousin, Tanner, turned their backs on Wright Media and were cut off from funds and cut out of wills because of it—not that it affected Tanner much because he has his own money after working for Wright Media for most of his career and making a name for himself in radio before he exited the company a few months ago, leaving a shit storm in his wake—and I don't want that for myself. Call me a sell-out, or even call me complicit. But I'm not giving up my ability to make a difference when I get to be in charge. Not when I've already waited this long and sacrificed two marriages along the way.

P.S. I'm only twenty-nine.

"Hmmm. Surely, I have something...flirtier to wear," I say to my reflection as I let out a sigh, knowing that isn't true because my wardrobe consists of workwear, sweats and pajamas. I'm almost thirty years old and it seems I've already given up on life after two failed attempts at marriage in my early twenties. The first one was a reckless mistake, but the second time, I thought I was signing up for the fairytale. What I got was a Stephen King novel instead. I swore I'd never go back there. Walking down that aisle a second time was singularly the worst choice I've ever made in my life. And after an even nastier divorce, I'd rather be perpetually single than risk that nightmare again. I've spent the last few years avoiding men and relationships like the plague. But then, my brother introduced me to a man named Banks and suddenly it feels like my resolve is slipping.

Maybe I could dip my toe in the water for a moment, maybe even take a short swim and still manage to come out unscathed?

The drag queen we're going to see, Coco Monroe, is Banks's cousin, and thanks to a connection the sweet girl my brother is dating has with this drag queen, I found myself invited along on a group outing. I don't get to see my brother a lot, so I jumped at the chance to spend some time with him and get to know this girl, Tahlia, he's so keen on. But when Banks expressed an interest in going too, well, I more than jumped, I practically did a backflip, some star jumps and a belly flop. The man is... *stunning*.

I don't think I've ever experienced a full-body reaction the first time I've met a man before. But when Banks turned that broad, confident smile and those warm, dark eyes my way, the only thing I could do was *giggle*. Oh, and flirt—something I haven't done in *so* long. It's like we had a moment just between us where all the noise in the room disappeared and we were the only ones there. I came away from it feeling all warm and trying not to smile too much, but I'm so eager to see him again. Even if it's just to see if I react to the bar owner the same way again.

Besides the fact that he's tall, dark skinned and deliciously handsome, I also love the fact that he's his own man. He owns a bar in the financial district called *Banked Up*. It's where all the wealthy Wall St brokers burn off some steam after a long day of trading other peoples' money. Very up-market. Constantly busy. And the kind of place that takes more smarts than luck to make successful. Needless to say, I'm impressed from the get go. And what I liked even more was that if he knew who my family is, he gave no indication. So, for once in my life, I'm going into an evening with a man without trepidation, because while money makes men attractive, for a woman, it's...different. In my experience, it made me a bit of a target. And I really, really, *really* don't want to feel like that again.

My phone buzzes on the vanity, snapping me out of my tumultuous trip down memory lane and up river into Hopesville. I look to see a message from Ash light up the screen—**Heading to the bar now.**

Deciding I don't have time to second guess my outfit anymore, I tap out a quick, **leaving soon,** response and cap my lipstick, dropping it in my clutch. Then I spray a little perfume in the air and walk through it on my way to put on my heels and head out, taking the elevator to the lobby of my building.

"Ms. Wright," the elderly concierge says, trying to keep his voice even. But there's no hiding the surprise in his tone.

I smile. "Unusual to see me out after dark, huh, Carl?" I say as I move toward him.

"It's wonderful to see you out after dark, Ms. Wright. Someone so young shouldn't spend all her time alone."

I laugh. "You sound like my mother. Are there any cars about?"

"I'll call one around for you." He touches the side of his earpiece and relays the message. "Enjoy your night."

"Thank you, Carl." With my heels clacking against the marbled lobby, I make my way to the revolving doors where the doorman greets me by name and gestures to the already waiting town car. Carl is excellent at his job and seems capable of producing anything you need out of thin air. This is why the man has a beautiful Rolex on his wrist. People will tip a man well for consistently coming through for them.

"Where to, miss?" the driver asks as I slide in.

"Banked Up," I instruct, sitting back against the gray leather seat with a happy sigh.

"Right away. Will you need a return car, miss?"

A soft smile tugs at the corners of my lips as the image of Banks smiling at me fills my mind and that little ball of maybe gets bigger. "I'm not sure," I say, looking out the window. "I think I might just see where tonight takes me."

BANKS

"I'll likely be gone a few hours," I say, checking my watch. "So, I might not get a chance to return before we close."

The bar manager nods. "Not a problem. I can handle anything that comes up. I think it's good that you're getting out yourself for a change," he says as he lifts a tray of glasses and adds it to the cooling system embedded in the bar. Everything tastes better in an ice-cold glass. "Now, quit hovering and go already. I'm sure your friends are waiting."

"I get it. I'm a workaholic. But I'm going now. Call me if you need anything."

"I won't," he calls out as I move out from behind the bar and make my way to the front of *Banked Up,* the upscale bar I've put my blood, sweat and tears into.

Years ago, when I bought this place, the guys I worked with on Wall Street thought I was absolutely insane. But I'd had enough of the cutthroat trading game by the time I was thirty and was more than ready to get out of it. I sunk everything I had into setting up and launching this bar, and while it was a gamble, I'm glad I took that risk. Almost a decade later, *Banked Up* is still the place to be for young professionals. And I couldn't be happier.

Taking a moment to greet a few regulars on my way out the door, I can't wipe the smile off my face because even though I love my work and rarely take time away, I'm looking forward to going somewhere different tonight. It's been a solid year since I've had the chance to go and see one of my cousin, Darren's, drag shows. From what I hear, he's been going from strength to strength and has landed himself a steady emceeing gig at *Queen's Delight* in Midtown East. I'm keen to see how much his character, Coco Monroe, and her show has grown. But despite my familial reasons for going out tonight there's also a personal reason. And her name is Isla.

Tall, beautiful, curvy, *busty* Isla.

I wanted her the moment I saw her. And I'm not the kind of man who refrains from going after what he wants. It's how I have always lived my life and it's what made me the man I am today. I'm not about to stop being me just because the woman I want is one of Wright Media's protégées with the power to tear down everything I hold dear with one well-targeted smear campaign. To me, the risk might be there should things go awry, but the reward in bedding such a powerful woman and seeing her vulnerable side is far greater in my opinion, and it makes me only want her more.

Not that who she is matters since the first thing I noticed was how my body reacted to her. And then I noticed the way she flirted with me. There was something familiar about that long dark hair and bright smile, but it wasn't until I was properly introduced that I realized she was Isla *Wright*, the youngest daughter of Paul Wright. Paul is one of three siblings who are well past their prime and sit at the helm of *Wright Media Corporation* with their children working one level down with a view to take over when the ancient ones—the term I like to use for old men who don't know when to retire—either die at their desk or step down over some scandal. Although, so far, the older Wright generation seem bulletproof. Even a public court battle between the oldest son and father didn't seem to rattle any cages. The Wrights are unstoppable. And I think the older generation will be running things for a long while yet.

Why do I know all these things as a bar owner, you ask? Well, my cousin's fiancé is Tanner Wright's brother-in-law—the son who forced his father to admit his wrongdoing and fully pay for his disabled sister's care—so, I have a smaller degree of separation to this powerful family than most, meaning I've googled them, fallen down a rabbit hole learning how insidious their media monopoly really is, and continued watching for any further rebellions from the next generation of Wrights as it becomes clearer and clearer that they may never get the chance to take over. It also means that not only do I find Isla Wright beautiful, I also find her intriguing since she's the only female in the generation to come. *What will her role be when the old men leave? Does she think they ever will? Are they considering a hostile takeover?*

"Banks! Come and have a drink with us," my buddy, Ronan—a venture capitalist—calls out as I pass, indicating that he's surrounded by a bunch of Wall St guys. Some of them I know from my time there.

"I'm just on my way out. But I'll catch up next time, OK?" I say over my shoulder as I make a break for the door and breathe a sigh of relief. Ronan has been my closest friend since middle school, and I have all the time in the world for him. But the Wall St guys? Them, I can pass on. There's a certain kind of arrogance to men who have more money than they'll ever know what to do with, and you can only handle them in small doses—I should know since I used to be one of them.

The moment I step onto the sidewalk to find freedom, a town car pulls up in front of me and none other than Isla Wright steps out from the back seat. I pause and smile, sliding my hands into my pockets as I watch the driver help her to her feet then drive away after she hands him a tip. I'm not sure she's even seen me yet, because she looks up at the neon sign for *Banked Up*, smiles to herself then takes a deep breath and starts to walk in. I grin at the sight. *Yeah, I'm looking forward to seeing you again too.*

"Isla," I say before she gets to the door, startling her. Her hand flies to her chest as her chocolate-brown eyes find mine.

"Banks! I didn't see you there. Hi." Her heels click on the pavement as she moves toward me, her skirt hugging her shapely thighs. "Are we meeting the others out here?"

I frown. "We're meant to be meeting them at *Queens Delight*."

"Oh god. I was so sure we said here. Lucky I ran into you then. It would have been embarrassing sitting inside alone all night waiting."

"I'm sure you wouldn't have been alone for long," I say, leaning in slightly. "A beautiful woman like you must be beating them off with a stick." She releases a hollow laugh and steps back.

"I can assure you that I haven't beaten *anybody* off for a long time," she says, sending my brows sky high before her eyes go wide, and her hand goes to her plum-colored mouth. "Oh my god. Please don't read into that. I just meant that I don't really date." That makes two of us. The older I get, it seems the less I have patience for anything lacking in substance. But from everything I know about Isla Wright so far, substance seems to be her defining quality. I must know her.

"Tell you what. I promise not to hold it against you, if you promise to come and have a drink with me before we go."

"I think I can handle a promise like that," she says. "But do we have the time? I don't want to be rude and walk in halfway through the show."

Glancing at my watch, I shake my head. "We won't be late. We've got a good hour before the show starts. So, I think that gives us plenty of time for a pre-game drink." I look into her eyes as she bites the inside of her lip in consideration. "Plus, it'll give us some time to get to know each other since we're the only two in the group who don't have a pre-existing friendship."

"Are you trying to be my friend, Banks?" she says with a teasing smile. My dick goes hard.

"Highly probable. Either that, or I'm just trying to talk you into my bed."

She laughs. "You're honest."

"It's the only way to be. So, about that drink."

Tucking her clutch purse under her arm, she moves toward me. "OK. Let's do it."

I gesture to a small door beside the bar. "Then let me take you somewhere quiet. I think tonight is about to get very noisy."

She follows me without pause. "Lead the way."

ISLA

"You know, I always had this pre-conceived notion that apartments above bars would be noisy and dingy. But this..." I stop moving, not even trying to conceal my obvious gawking as I absorb the bright and airy space. "This is stunning."

His furnishings are simple and sleek—black leather couch in the living area with rustic wooden furnishings that are a shade or two darker than the wood-paneled floor; marble countertops in the kitchen with stainless steel appliances and LED lighting creating an ambient glow around the base of his cupboards, along with great big floor to ceiling windows that highlight the hustle and bustle of the city down below. But most of all, the thing I notice most about this space is the quiet. I can't even feel the vibration of the music in the bar coming up through the floor. It's like we're in another world.

"Some say I have a well-trained eye," Banks says as he hands me a crystal glass with clear liquid and a lime wedge inside. "Vodka and tonic." His fingers remain wrapped around the tumbler for a moment longer than they should, ensuring lasting contact between our fingers as I take it from him. I suck in and hold my breath. Something about this man crowding my space and making his intentions abundantly clear sets off every nerve ending in my body. Which in itself is an odd feeling. I'm surrounded by bossy, overbearing men in almost every other aspect of my life. Being a Wright means that every action or decision I make runs through the echelons of our patriarchal family. And if the old men at the top don't like it, they wield whatever power they have over you to pull you back into line. So, naturally, I'm opposed to any sort of controlling or bossy behavior. But then, Banks isn't being bossy or controlling, he's being *assertive* and perhaps pre-emptive of my needs. And *that,* ladies and gentlemen, is the difference between an alpha, and an asshole who *thinks* he's an alpha.

"Thank you," I murmur, lifting the glass to my lips as I smile, both at the innuendo in his initial comment and my thoughts following. For the first time in a very long time, I can actually see myself getting naked with something other than my battery operated stand-ins.

Banks is intoxicating, which means I need to be careful here too. Smart women should *never* trust an intoxicating man with her heart. She's likely to get squashed and feel stupid when she's left alone and heartbroken in the morning. I put my mental guards up.

"A seat?" With his eyes on my lips and throat as he watches me swallow, he inclines his head toward the big leather couch that sits across from a flickering fire that seems to be there more for the ambience than the warmth.

I walk ahead and position myself in the far corner, crossing my legs and balancing my glass on my knee. He sits not far from me, mirroring my position in a way that makes my grin even bigger. *This guy is good.* I feel like I'm the center of his world right now and can't help but wonder how many women he's done exactly this with previous to me.

"Tell me about the bar," I start, lifting my glass and sipping while maintaining eye contact—I can play games too.

"What do you want to know?"

"How did it come about? It's obviously a play on your name, but how did you know it'd become as popular as it is?"

He chuckles as he lifts his drink to his mouth. "I didn't." Taking a small sip, he hisses slightly as he swallows and sets the glass back on his crossed knee, same as me.

"Are you telling me you set that place up without any sort of market research behind your decisions, and it just...worked out for you?"

"That's exactly what I'm telling you. I used to be a venture capitalist, so I know what works and what doesn't. And I was great at that, but..." He blows out a breath as he shakes his head slightly. "There was just something kind of hollow about making money for the sake of making money off the ideas of someone else. And I'd had this idea for a bank-themed cocktail bar in the financial district for years, so I did what I do best, and I took a gamble."

"And didn't look back?" I finish for him, and he nods.

"Not for a second. I mean, there were a few moments in the beginning where I wondered if I was stone-cold crazy sinking everything I had into a bar when I didn't have any experience owning one. But I figured, I've been poor before, so if I fell on my face, I already knew how to survive. I knew how to build myself up from nothing, so the risk wasn't really that high. The gain, however"—he looks around his apartment and a half-smile curves his mouth, giving me a glimpse of the proud man he's become—"was worth it."

"I think you'd get along well with my cousin, Tanner," I say with a sigh. "He's the big risk taker in the Wright family."

"What about your brother? Ash, right? I don't see his name anywhere on the company register."

My eyebrows shoot up. "Been doing some investigating?"

"Family is very important to me, Isla, and since my cousin is closely involved with multiple members of the Wright family, I make it my business to know who all the stakeholders are."

"That's fair. Although now I'm feeling a little underprepared because I didn't study up on you. But then, I did step out in public with you for five minutes, so I'm sure my father's spies already have an entire dossier written up about you, weighing up the pros and cons of any sort of affiliation with each other."

"Sounds like...freedom," Banks says with a laugh.

"Oh, it's not that bad. I'm exaggerating, of course. They only create dossiers if something like marriage is on the table. Then they'll talk to us about that person's *potential*." He smirks at that. "For the most part, it's a pretty cushy existence. I show up to work, I jump through the hoops and the rest of the time, I'm left pretty much alone."

"As long as you don't do anything to piss off the patriarchy?" I laugh in response as he drains his glass then nods his head toward mine. "Another?"

I tilt my glass to the side, noting there's nothing but a little ice and the lime wedge left inside it. "I shouldn't. We should probably just go. Everyone will be waiting on us."

I stand and Banks stands with me, taking the glass from between my fingers. "Or," he starts, his rich brown eyes drinking in every inch of my face as he towers over me. "We could stay. Just a little longer."

And as his eyes lock with mine, they hold so much promise that I find myself nodding along. "I guess one more drink can't hurt."

ISLA

Alcohol and regret are common bedfellows indeed, and it's the former that leads one to the latter. My inevitable tumble into Banks Johnson's bed is no exception to this rule.

It starts with tension—all great hookups do—then it's followed by wonderful conversation that makes me feel heard and understood in a way I rarely am. Conversation so good that I keep accepting those offered drinks, completely forgetting the time until that tension is all there is and suddenly, it's imperative we both act.

I don't even know who leans in first. But what I am certain of is that the moment our lips touch, everything else just falls away and all there is left in this world is the sensation of his mouth and tongue moving against mine while our bodies collide, pulling each other closer and closer until I'm lifted off the couch and carried into what I'm guessing is a bedroom as lush as the rest of his apartment. But it's not the furnishings I'm looking at. No. It's the man holding himself above me, pulling his shirt over his head and revealing a rippling chest that makes my mouth water and my insides clench.

The only thought in my head is *want,* and the only feeling I experience is *need*, and as he pushes my skirt up around my hips and pulls my panties down my legs, the only word I can say is, "*Yes.*" Because right now—as Banks's mouth connects with my apex—I don't have a solitary regret.

"Fuck me, you taste good," he moans, his tongue gliding through my seam before he centers his focus on my clit, licking and sucking and teasing my already intoxicated mind to such heights I might not be able to remember my name if asked.

His fingertips circle my entrance as his hot breath washes over my inner thigh. "You smell amazing too," he rasps, dragging his teeth against my tender skin before he inserts his fingers and covers my clit with his mouth yet again.

"Keep going."

"I have no intention of stopping," he whispers, nipping lightly at my inner thigh before diving back in, sliding two long, thick fingers inside me as he sucks and swirls, working me into a frenzy.

My hands clench against the bedsheets, my back arching high as I moan and shudder, spiraling toward my imminent climax. "Oh god. Yes! Yes, Banks! Yes! *Banks!*" As my orgasm rips through me, my hips lift off the bed, my thighs closing around Banks's face as I ride out the wave, fucking his face and fingers like it might be the last sexual experience I ever have. It's too good and too much all at once, and when my body feels like it might burst into flames, I place my hand against his forehead and gasp, "Enough. Enough."

"Mmm," he moans, curling his arms around my thighs as his tongue rapidly flicks my bundle of nerves, sending me over the edge when I honestly thought I couldn't take anymore.

I howl up at the ceiling like a wolf calling to its pack, and if it ends up that a bunch of wolves take to the streets of New York, then we'll all know who's to blame. Not that I could give a damn even if I wanted to. My brain is total mush and my body is nothing more than humming pleasure impulses as Banks does things to my body no one—not even myself—has done to me before. The man has a magic mouth and artist's fingers, and if he turned around and told me I had to pay him after this, I'd probably just hand him my keycard and tell him he's welcome to whatever he wants. Pleasure like this is absolutely priceless.

"On your knees." Banks's deep voice rumbles out a command that my liquified brain has no choice but to obey. He could tell me to do a handstand against the wall so he could fuck me upside down and I'd oblige. There's literally nothing I wouldn't do in this moment if it means feeling this good for as long as possible.

"Fuck me. Fuck me," I beg, keening noises coming out of me as I sway on my knees, urging my hips back toward him. "Please. I want you inside me."

"And you'll get it," he rasps, placing his big hand in the center of my back before he drags his fingers down my spine until he's cupping my ass and humming as if that smooth pale skin is all he ever wanted. "I'm just trying to decide whether I'm going to survive this."

"I'll resuscitate you, if need be," I say over my shoulder, flashing him a smile as he takes his cock in hand then circles it around my entrance.

"You might need to," he hisses, pushing a little inside and stretching me around his girth.

I gasp out a moan, my entire body singing with the sweet torture of opening up for him. He's bigger than I anticipated, but holy hell, it feels good.

"So. Tight." Banks's words sound like they're being forced through gritted teeth. "So. Good."

"Yes. Oh yes! Give it to me, *please*."

Banks pulls his hips back and drives into me harder in response, his hand sliding up my back and grabbing the now messed-up curls as a way to lever himself in as deep as possible. I cry out as my head reefs back. Not from pain, but from absolute pleasure. With each measured thrust, I'm filled to depths I couldn't have possibly fathomed before. Every nerve is alive, and even my nipples are tingling like they have an orgasm of their own to give up too. I've never been so...*aroused* and turned on before.

"Fuck me," Banks growls, his thrusts getting faster and more erratic. "I can't. I can't...hold. *Fuuuuck!*"

With a final pivot, he buries himself all the way and pulses deep inside me, triggering my reciprocal release and a deep, long moan.

"Whoa," I gasp as we both collapse onto our backs and stare up at the ceiling. "That was..." I can't find the words.

"I know." Banks swipes a hand down his face as his chest heaves for breath. "That was definitely whoa."

"Something tells me we missed Darren's show," I say, catching sight of the neon red numbers on Banks's bedside clock.

"I'll make it up to him." Banks turns to me and smiles. "And to you, well, it looks like we have a bit more time together."

Sitting up, I slide my legs off the bed and take a deep inhale, swallowing past the dryness in my throat as I shake my head and try to find my panties on the floor. "I don't think that's such a great idea," I say as I catch them up in my fingers and slide them past my feet.

"You're leaving me?" He rolls to his side and lifts his brow like he can't believe this is actually happening.

"Regrettably, yes," I say, standing as I shimmy into my panties and pull my skirt back down. "As much fun as 'getting to know you' was, Mr. Banks. I kind of think it'd be in both of our best interests to end it right here."

"*Both* of our interests?" he repeats with a laugh. "And it's just Banks. After I plowed you into my mattress only seconds ago, I think we're way past formalities."

"You have a bit of a dirty mouth, don't you?" I say, grinning as I tuck my blouse in straight and run my fingers through my messy hair.

"Get back into bed and I'll show you just how dirty I can be." His grin is so inviting as he taps the mattress that I almost give in. *Almost.* But I've danced this dance enough times to know when a man is no good for me, and as it turns out, the greater the chemistry in the beginning, the bigger the crash in the end. I don't know about the rest of the population, but for me, I'm just not willing to put my heart on the line again. I'd rather have my fun and walk away with my dignity still intact.

"As tempting as that offer is," I say, sliding my feet back into my heels, "I'm standing by my initial decision." I straighten up and place my hands on my hips as I let my gaze run over his long, toned body one last time. My insides clench and beg me to reconsider, but my brain and my heart know better. I hold out my hand. "Thank you for the drinks—plural. And for the good time, Banks. It was...memorable."

He rakes his top teeth over his bottom lip, smiling like he can't believe I'm actually walking away from a specimen as fine as him—and honestly, I'm struggling with the decision too. But I know what's best for me, and that's definitely not him. The very fact I fell into bed with him instead of meeting an obligation I had to show up to an outing with my brother and his new girlfriend means he's got trouble written all over him. I could completely ruin myself over a man like Banks Johnson. So, the best thing for me to do is to get far, far away from here with one great memory to keep me company.

"What if I just buy you dinner?" he says instead of taking my outstretched hand. "Feeding you before you leave is the least I can do."

"You don't owe me anything. I can feed myself."

He sucks air in through his teeth as he chuckles and reaches out to shake my hand finally. "In that case, *Ms.* Wright. I'll bid you adieu." Sighing with a smile of relief, I go to remove my hand but his grip only tightens. "But one of these days, Isla, you're gonna have to let someone into that self-sufficient heart of yours. Maybe it's not me, and maybe it's not today, or even tomorrow. But eventually, you'll have to let those walls of yours down."

"Maybe I just like being on my own," I reply, practically whispering as he releases my hand and I pull it back, my skin still tingling.

He rolls onto his back and chuckles, giving me a beautiful view of his half-erect manhood as the city lights push in through the windows and highlight his skin. "No one likes being alone, Isla," he says, his eyes locking with mine as I take a deep breath and nod instead of providing an answer.

"Thanks again, Banks," I say, backing out the door as I push his insights down as deep as they can go. Seems Banks just did a lot more than just fuck me better than I've ever been fucked before. Somehow, he saw right through me too. And I've never felt more naked.

BANKS

"Hey, man," Ronan says, when I venture down to the bar about thirty minutes later, needing to get out of my far-too-quiet apartment after my night ended sooner than expected. "Manager said you'd be out for the night. Hot date gone bad?" He smiles jovially and claps me on the back. But I don't really feel like laughing. He kind of hit the nail on the head.

"Not bad. Just... over before I wanted it to end. Which is weird. That doesn't normally happen to me."

He furrows his brow slightly as he nods. "Well, if it becomes a problem, you know a doctor can help you with that, right?"

It takes me a minute to realize what the hell he's going on about before I roll my eyes and scoff. "Not *that* kind of problem. Fuck, Ronan. I'm thirty-eight, not seventy-fucking-eight."

Ronan chuckles as he lifts his glass of Grey Goose on the rocks and drinks. "Hey, I've heard of that shit happening to guys as young as *twenty*-eight. Stress of the job." He bounces a shoulder. "It's not for everyone."

"Yeah. Well, when you're working on Wall St. I can understand it." I lift my eyes to meet his mossy-green gaze and shrug. "But away from that life, I'm pretty fucking stress free."

He releases a slow breath and shakes his blond head slowly, looking at me in bewilderment. "I just don't understand how you did it."

A server brings me over a vodka tonic, and I thank her. "Did what?"

"Walk away from it all. The adrenaline rush. The feeling of power when you make the call of the century. I don't think I could give that up for anyone or anything. I thrive under pressure."

"And yet, you're the guy with the knowledge about limp dick doctors," I retort, eyebrows raised.

He rolls his eyes and laughs. "You're a real asshole, you know? Anyone ever told you that before?"

"A handful of times," I say with a chuckle. "So, besides your broken dick, how's everything going."

"For the record, my dick is perfectly fine. Work is too. I'm actually up for promotion. If all goes well this month, I'll be heading up my own division. And you know what that means?"

"A fuck ton of stress and giant bonuses if your team delivers."

"Fuckin' A. It's everything I've been working toward. Not a single person from the old neighborhood will ever be able call me a loser wannabe again."

I look at him for a long moment, remembering the skinny little kid who struggled harder than any other kid in the neighborhood. We became friends in middle school when I started splitting my lunch with him before my mom realized and started packing enough for two. Ronan Kennedy might have an important family's surname, but he certainly didn't get a lot of the privilege that should come with it. Anything he has, he fought hard for. The kid with little to no food in his belly creates an adult who's perpetually hungry for more, more and more. And I often wonder at what point it will be enough. What will he end up sacrificing before he's sated?

"What neighborhood?" I say, placing my hand on his right shoulder. "I don't think there's a single person still living there who should matter to either one of us anymore. All the important people are out. So anything we do now, it's for us. We ain't got nothing to prove, man. We both made it the day we got accepted into college."

"I know you're right. But I just...I don't think I'm

finished yet. Like, I haven't climbed to the top of my mountain."

"OK." I raise my glass. "Then here's to finding what's at the top of that mountain."

He taps his glass to mine. "Hopefully it's a big pot of gold," he jokes, taking a drink.

"And then what?" I say suddenly, causing him to freeze and frown like he doesn't understand the question.

"What do you mean?"

"What happens when you're at the top of the mountain with your pot of gold? Is that just…it?"

"Nah, man. That's when I get to do whatever I want. Everyone knows the best part about climbing a hill is sledding back down. So imagine how much fun it'll be sitting on that pot of gold then sliding back down that mountain."

Pausing for a moment, I ponder his words as my mind wanders along the journey of my life until now. I've worked my way from nothing up to something, and then I turned that something into an icon with this bar. But now what? Now that I've made a success of everything I've put my mind to, where do I go now?

The answer comes in flashes, memories of smiles and gasps as I remember everything about my evening with Isla. And that's when it hits me.

"I think I want to get married and have kids," I state, causing Ronan to choke on his drink.

"You *what?*"

"Yeah," I say, nodding to myself as my mind takes hold of the idea with both hands. "I think this place is the peak of my mountain. It's time for me to head back down the other side. I want to take a step back and start a family."

"With who?"

"That part's to be decided, my friend. But I have a pretty solid idea."

"The date who left early tonight?"

I nod. "I've just gotta get her to lower her walls enough to let me in. Prove to her I'm the man she needs."

"Because that's the *easy* part," he says with a sarcastic laugh.

"Well, I haven't met an obstacle I couldn't overcome. So whatever is in Isla Wright's past that made her think we were a bad idea, I intend to find out."

"Wait. The girl you want to settle down with is Isla *Wright?* As in Wright Media?" I nod. "Fuck, man," he says, waving to the waitress to bring over another round. "You're either insane, or you've got the biggest balls out of anyone I know. That family is old money. They could eat you alive."

"Lucky I'm only interested in the daughter," I say, downing the last of my drink as my resolution sets in.

LSLA

"There are flowers on your desk," Karen, my assistant and favorite all-round person, says when I get into the office Monday morning. "I'm guessing you had an interesting weekend."

"Never as interesting as yours, I'm sure," I say, entering my office and immediately spotting the arrangement of flowers in a variety of purple and pink shades that sits in a beautiful vase at the corner of my desk. They smell amazing.

"Read the card! There's a card," Karen says, bouncing on her toes as she clasps her iPad to her chest and waits for me to round my desk.

"It's probably just from a client whose ass I saved with a well-timed article and a positive spin glossing over their bad behavior," I say, plucking the card from the stand.

Karen smiles knowingly. "I don't think so."

I flick open the card and my heart hammers out a cheek-heating rhythm as flashes of memory—tongues on skin, fingers in hair and *thrust, thrust, thrust*—take over my mind. I have to close my eyes and place a steadying hand on my desk before I can even pretend I didn't just experience a bunch of after tremors from the best sex I've ever had.

"What does it say?" Karen asks, her pointer finger pushing her glasses up her nose as her brown eyes go wide with eagerness.

"Ah." I clear my throat. "Just a thank you card…uh…from a client. As expected." I slide the card back inside the tiny envelope and tuck it under the base of the vase.

"I think they're from a suitor," Karen says. "But if you don't want to share whatever made you blush like you've been sitting in the sun too long with your very best friend in the world, then I'm not going to force you. I can respect your privacy."

"Thank you," I say, breathing a sigh of relief as I sit in my chair. "It really is no big deal."

"Obviously," she says, moving a little closer as her grip tightens on the iPad. "I guess it's just been so long since you've been on a date that you're out of practice. So of *course* you're going to blush when a man thanks you for a nice evening. I mean, it's not like he thinks the plum-colored orchids remind him of your lips, right?"

I gasp and sit ramrod straight. "You *read* it!"

"Me? Never." She places a delicate hand on her chest and feigns innocence. "Why, it's just a guess that the purple are for your mouth and the pink are for... well, parts he probably shouldn't name."

My mouth and eyes both widen as I suck in a breath and try to decide whether I want to dissolve into a puddle of nothingness or pitch a fit and fire her on the spot. Although, we both know I'd never, ever fire her. Not only is she my bestie, but she's also the best damn PA I've ever had. The woman is invaluable and puts up with all of the Wright family political drama like a champ.

"So...who's the lucky guy?" she asks, waggling her eyebrows as I look at her through parted fingers.

"No one," I moan.

"Well, 'no one' has a bit of a mouth on him." She picks up the card and reads over Banks's words again, sighing like she's in the middle of a swoony romance novel. "Kind of reminds me of Andy in the beginning of our relationship. He used to leave me notes like this. He works at Starbucks, so he'd write them on the side of my coffee cup." She places the card back on my desk and smiles. "Those were the days."

"Wh-what did he write?" I ask, knowing I'm likely to regret my words the moment they fall from my mouth. Karen and her live-in boyfriend, Andy, have a peculiar relationship. When you first see them together, it kind of seems like they hate each other. But then you realize that they both get off on their weird dynamic, and then you just realize they're super freaky.

"Well there were a *lot* but my favorite was when he wrote, 'Tonight's safe word is bananas' because when I went to his place that night, he had a *huge* banana that he used to fu—"

"La-la-la!" I stick my fingers in my ears. "I'm sorry I asked! I knew it was a bad idea, but..."

Karen laughs and pushes off the side of my desk. "I'm just happy you got laid well enough that you're still flushed thinking about it," she says. "It's been far too long in between men."

"It was nice and all. But it was just a one-time thing," I say, taking the card and putting it in my top drawer.

"If you say so," she says, looking like she doesn't believe a word I'm spouting as she heads for the door. "And by the way, you've got about thirty minutes before you're expected to meet with your father and uncles."

I groan. "Did the invite say what it was about?"

"Nope. And you're the only one invited, so I'm guessing they already know about your new man."

"No. They can't know about him. They'll want to know why I went to lunch with Ash." I sit back in my chair and groan. *God I hate my family.*

"I'll have a stiff drink waiting for when you return." She widens her eyes dramatically as she slips out of my office and closes the door, leaving me alone with the fragrant bouquet of flowers and the well-worded card sent by Banks Johnson himself.

With an unsteady breath, I pull the card out of my desk again, scanning over the neat handwriting and the phone number at the bottom. I get stuck on that number. My thumbnail between my teeth as I contemplate tapping it into the keypad and hearing the silky voice that's filled my dreams for the last couple of nights. *Maybe it wouldn't be as bad this time?*

The moment the thought enters my mind, I shove the card back in my drawer and close my eyes, shaking away the urge for more as quickly as it starts. While one night with Banks Johnson promises another will be just as good, I know myself well enough to hit the brakes before we're moving so fast we end up crashing into a wall—or worse, married. And since I've made that mistake twice already, the lesson I've learned is that Isla Wright and relationships don't mix. Like my father and his half dozen failed marriages, I'm better off alone.

BANKS

"So...what happened to you on Friday night?" Tahlia asks at the start of her Thursday shift, the little redhead's voice dripping with hopeful curiosity.

"Nothing," I say from behind the bar. It's about thirty minutes before the doors open, and I'm just doing my usual, checking everything is stocked and ready to go. Sure, I have employees for all of this, but I'm a hands-on guy, and I find that participating in set up and close shows my workers that I'm willing to do the things I ask them to do. It sets us up for a better working relationship.

"Nothing?" She leans on the bar and smiles up at me. "You missed your cousin's show for *nothing?*"

Pausing what I'm doing, I meet Tahlia's blue eyes and maintain a stony expression. We may be friendly with each other—she's very close with my cousin, Darren, who is the reason I hired her in the first place—but it doesn't mean that I owe her any explanations for how I choose to spend my time. Hell, I don't explain myself to *anyone*. So, despite the fact that she's friends with a family member while also dating the brother of the woman I'm interested in, she doesn't get any details. Those kinds of things are private, and whatever goes on between Isla and me from this point on, stays between us. Especially since I've sent her two lots of flowers and an invitation to dinner in the last week, and I've received nothing in return.

"I'll make things right with Darren. I simply got caught up." *In your boyfriend's sister...* I feel my dick twitch as a sliver of a memory hits my consciousness. Then I squash it back down as fast as I can so I don't end up with a full-blown hard on in front of my staff.

Tahlia keeps pace beside me when I make a break for the storeroom. "Interesting that Isla was missing on Friday, too."

"Why would that be interesting?" I ask, grabbing a box of cocktail napkins and attempting to return to the bar, only to be blocked by the tiny cocktail waitress.

"I don't know. I guess after witnessing the air-gasm you two had just looking at each other last Friday when you met, I kind of thought the fact neither of you showed might mean something."

"Air-gasm?" I scoff, pushing past her with an excuse me. Of course she follows.

"Yeah. The charge in the air when you locked eyes, and if that wasn't enough for Ash and me to pick up on, you let a couple of sexually charged innuendos fly too. It was pretty obvious the only reason you two agreed to come out was because you wanted to see each other again."

I grunt a response as I put the napkins in the holders behind the bar.

"So, what happened? Did you both arrive at the same time then decide to go make your own fun? Or did you arrange to meet up secretly without us?" She grins as she follows me along on the opposite side of the bar. "Come on, Banks. You can tell me. I won't tell anyone else."

I let out a laugh at that one. "Except maybe Darren, who'll tell Theo, who'll tell Ruby, who'll tell Tanner, who'll mention it to Isla. *Or*, you'll say something to Ash who will go directly to Isla and ask her what's going on." I shake my head as I finish with the napkins and start breaking down the empty box. "No thank you. I'll keep my personal life personal thanks."

"No problem," Tahlia says as she steps away and giggles. "You just told me everything I wanted to know anyway."

"What?" I gape, quickly running over what I said

and realizing that by trying to say nothing, I actually admitted I was with Isla inadvertently. "Shit."

"It's OK," she says, reaching across the bar and patting my hand. "I give you my word that no one—not even Ash or Darren—will hear anything from me."

"I appreciate your confidentiality. Especially since nothing is actually going on between us."

Her brows go up. "Got it out of your system already then, huh? I really thought there'd be something more to it than one night."

Pressing my lips together, I inhale a deep breath. "Me too, Tahlia," I say, before I rap my knuckles against the bar then excuse myself to head toward the office where I can be done with this conversation and have a moment of quiet before service starts. I need to regroup. Wooing Isla via traditional means doesn't seem to be working. So if I want anything more than just one night with her, I'm going to have to get creative. But what does a man offer when a woman has the means to give herself everything a person in this world could ask for?

ISLA

"No flowers today, huh?" Karen says in my doorway as we finish up work. After receiving two bunches of flowers within days of each other, I do have to agree that it felt like it was becoming a habit. But since Wednesday's bunch was accompanied by a note inviting me to dinner on Friday night—to which I declined—it does seem that Banks has realized he's barking up the wrong tree. I'm not sure if I'm elated or disappointed. Because I wanted this, right? I wanted to have my night and walk away with no regrets.

So what's that weird feeling in the pit of my stomach then?

"Can't blame the guy for quitting his pursuit. It's kind of a relief, really," I say, standing up and putting on my coat while my computer shuts down at the end of a long Monday.

"Pity," she says, looking at her nails. "I was kinda hoping this guy would work a little harder and chip away at the grumpy 'I'm better off on my own' façade you've got going on." She deepens her voice at one point, making it out like I'm some kind of craggy bear.

"I don't think I sound like that." I laugh.

"Close enough. All that wound licking has deepened your voice."

"You're so hilarious," I say, picking up my bag and heading for the door. She steps out of the way.

"It's a gift. Maybe I could convince Coco Monroe to give me a go on stage. I think I'd make a stunning drag queen."

"Aren't drag queens all men?"

"Oh no, a woman can dress in drag. It's a style—a character—and I happen to think I'd be amazing."

"OK. So what would your drag name be?"

She thinks on that for a moment as we leave my office and pause by her desk while she grabs her things. "That's a tough one. It'd have to be something that reflects my inner self. Oh! I've got it," she says, finger in the air like an exclamation point. "Donna Matrix. I'd wear skintight leather, spike-heeled boots, shiny red lipstick with heavily winged eye makeup and a long, red ponytail that I can whip around like a cat of nine tails."

"That sounds horrifying," I say, chuckling over the

image she just conjured in my head as we step onto the elevator.

"It sounds exciting," she points out. "And when I get home, I'm going to tell Andy my idea. I'll bet he'll want to act that out as soon as possible. Why, just the other day, I had to take his ball gag out because he had—"

"No, no, no!" I wave my hands in the air, thankful she and I are the only ones left working at this hour, so the elevator cab is empty save for us two. "The moment the words ball and gag are linked together, I can't listen anymore."

"You are so unfun." She pouts, although I know she's not really upset with me. Slipping in dirty Andy anecdotes and watching me react is probably her favorite sport.

"Just call me nana and leave me to my puzzles," I say as we hit the ground floor and step out into the lobby. "I honestly prefer solitude, Netflix and a thousand tiny pieces of cardboard to keep my company."

"So, hot bar owners wearing tailored pants and a gorgeous fucking vest don't even register on your radar?" she says, making me frown since that was an oddly descriptive comment.

"Well, no. I mean, sure, we had a great night, but I'm allowed to have it just be that. I'm allowed to choose singledom."

"Sure, sure," she says, nodding as we move past

security and say goodnight. "You should probably make a beeline to your car in that case. Because I think you've already registered on *his* radar."

"What?" I ask, glancing at Karen who points over my shoulder as we step onto the sidewalk. And right into Banks. "Holy fucking hell! Where did you come from?"

"I tried to warn you," Karen says, reaching around me with her hands out. "Nice to meet you, sir. You are stunning, by the way."

Banks smiles and my entire reproductive system takes notice. "Thank you, ma'am. The name's Banks. You are?" He shakes her hand and Karen's grin is so huge, I know she's never going to rest until Banks gets one of those chances she thinks I should be giving him.

"Karen. I'm Isla's bestie. We work together too. I'm her PA."

"Ah, the woman who controls the schedule. Perhaps it's you I should be asking to slot me in for a date." He leans in and gives Karen a conspiratorial wink, making Karen giggle.

"Oh, I can get you an audience with the boss anytime you want," she says. "You just give me a call, and I'll make it happen."

"I'll do that," he says, tapping the side of his nose.

"Are you two for real?" I say, looking between the two of them. "Number one, I'm right here. And number two, I can make my own dinner plans."

"She really can't," Karen puts in. "She eats take out probably six days out of the week."

"Because I don't like to cook. What's the harm in that?" I ask, arms out to the side.

"I can cook," Banks says, turning his attention to me. "And I've got a fully stocked kitchen. Any night of the week, I'll step away from the club and cook you a meal that'll make you wonder how you ever got by without me." *I've been wondering that since you made me come three times in a row last week.*

My breath thickens and I have to shake the lusty haze from my thoughts. This isn't happening.

"I'm fine eating chow mien noodles and satay as my main sustenance. Now, if you'll excuse me, my car is here."

I step to the side and head for the car only a few feet away with my driver waiting beside it. "It was lovely to run into you, Banks. *Good night,* Karen."

Karen giggles and gives me a finger wave as she steps away, miming to Banks that he should call her and she'll write him in the diary. I slap a hand over my face. *She's incorrigible!*

Banks chuckles and moves to open my door for me, nodding politely at the driver who steps out of the way. "She's a hoot."

"She thinks she's hilarious," I say, dropping my purse into the backseat before I turn back to Banks who still has that gorgeous, ovary-stimulating smile on his handsome face. "What are you doing here, Banks?"

He bounces a shoulder. "I was walking by."

"At the exact moment I decided to call it a night?" I glance at my watch and it's close to seven-twenty. Not a normal clock-off time.

"What can I say? I'm a lucky guy."

"*Or,* you're taking up stalking as a hobby."

"Oh, I'm sure no man could get close to you if you weren't willing to let him in, Isla Wright."

Something about the way he leans in and his voice lowers to an intimate level sends delighted chills all over my body. I lower my eyes before I look back up at him. "That's because I prefer solitude, Mr. Banks," I say as I slide into the car, tucking my legs inside and smiling back at him. "Have a nice evening."

"You too, Ms. Wright." He grins and places his hand on the top of the car door. "You know, I'm not going away."

"That's your choice, I suppose," I say, trying to quiet the thundering of my heart.

"I'm also going to wear you down. One day, I'll be sitting in that car right beside you."

"You seem very sure of yourself, Mr. Banks."

"Just Banks. But you already know that," he says, giving me a wink before he steps away and closes me in.

"Everything OK, ma'am?" the driver asks before we set off.

"Yeah," I say, realizing I'm slightly out of breath. "Everything's just fine."

And as we pull away from the curb, I find myself unable to take my eyes off the waiting Banks, standing on the curve with his hands in his pockets until we just can't see each other anymore. I don't fail to notice the way my heart responds. It's like I miss him even though he isn't mine to begin with.

BANKS

"Oh, now he turns up," Darren says when I arrive at his apartment at eleven the next day. He knew I was coming. We'd organized this brunch a week ago when I called to apologize for not going to his show. But, in a true Darren style, he needs to give me shit for it. "Only about 250 hours too late, but hey, you made it. Well done, cousin." He pats me on the back as I walk through the door.

"Don't listen to the drama queen," Theo, Darren's fiancé says as I shrug off my coat. "He didn't even notice you weren't at the show because he was too busy lapping up all the attention from his audience. I honestly think you could have not apologized and he wouldn't have even thought about it."

"Take that back, you cheeky man who's giving away all of my secrets," Darren teases, feigning an indignant gasp while he leads me to the little table in their kitchen. It's one of those old farmhouse ones with the weathered wood and faded paint. They also have mismatched chairs that add to the aesthetic. It's topped off with a lace table runner and a galvanized watering can with a bunch of flowers stuck into it. The only thing separating this from a suburban housewife's kitchen is the nipple tassel that's dangling off the watering can's spout.

"I speak truth," Theo says with a shrug from where he's standing, stirring something at the stove. "I don't know any other way to be."

"And it's one of the things I love about you," Darren says with a smile as they exchange an intimate glance before Theo turns my way.

"How's the bar?" he asks, glancing up from his stirring. "You want coffee?"

"Yes to coffee," I say. "And the bar is great. Kind of runs itself these days."

"Uh oh," Darren starts, carrying a tray with a French press and ceramic mugs to the table. "That sounds like a man looking for something."

"I'm fine," I say, sitting where he gestures. "I guess I'm just a little restless."

"Are you thinking of moving on? Finding a new challenge?" Darren asks as he presses down the plunger then starts pouring delicious smelling coffee into the three mugs.

I shake my head. "I don't want to move on. I love the bar. It's seriously my pride and joy, and I can't imagine not being the person who runs it. But, you know..." With the bounce of my shoulder, I add some cream to the mug Darren pushes my way then stir in half a spoonful of sugar.

"No, actually," Darren says. "We don't know. So you'll have to enlighten us." He waggles his drawn-on eyebrows above his coffee cup as he takes a swig.

I sigh. "I want to settle down and have a family," I admit, expecting Darren's eyes to bug out but instead noting a quiet understanding inside them.

He sets his coffee on the table and nods slowly. "That's understandable," he says.

I rub a hand over my face and shake my head, looking out the window as I try to find understanding myself. I've always been happy with my life, happy in my own company. I enjoy that feeling of freedom where I didn't have to answer to anyone or take anyone else's feelings into consideration whenever I made a decision. But now, it's like all I can do is think, 'How would Isla react to this?' 'What would she like to do today?' 'How is she feeling?' 'What is she doing?' 'What can I do to make her life better?' 'Does she have a favorite color?' and 'If I paint my walls that favorite color would she be more likely to stay?' The internal monologue seems endless and focused on only one thing. Making Isla mine.

"I'm glad *you* understand it," I say, half muttering against my hand.

"What's not to understand? We're all getting on in life—some more than others," he says, his eyes moving over me to point out that there's a five year difference in our age. I'm the one at the higher end at thirty-eight. "And it's natural to trade career goals for life goals. We all want someone to spend our nights with, to grow old with, to have children and grandchildren with."

"I don't even know if she wants children," I blurt, going stock-still when I register what I just said.

"*She?*" Darren gawks. "You're *dating?* Who, pray tell, is *she?*"

"Might as well give up the information now," Theo says as he brings over three plates of eggs benedict on toasted bagels with a spinach and rocket salad on the side. "Darren is nothing if not relentless when it comes to gleaning information. He'll cyberstalk you if that's what it takes. So put the poor guy out of his misery. Actually, put *me* out of any future misery, because you know he drags me along during all his hijinks."

"You love my hijinks," Darren says as he taps Theo against the chest.

"It's true," he says with a nod. "I'll do anything as long as he's smiling."

"And that's what I want," I say, thanking Theo for the food. "I want someone to smile with and to spend quality time with. What's the point of all this success if I don't have anyone to share it with?"

"I agree, I agree," Darren says. "But you still haven't said who this woman is. I'm waiting here with Facebook on my screen ready to stalk away." He turns his cell to me so I can see he's serious.

"Isla Wright," I say, biting the bullet and just laying it all out there. In my life, Darren has been the closest non-immediate family I've had considering we were both sent to live with our gran when our respective parents decided we needed 'straightening out'. My straightening was based on the trouble I was getting in once I got to high school, and Darren's was the fact he kept getting caught raiding his mother's shoes and makeup. One of these things was not like the other, and one of those things could not, and should never have even *tried* to be changed. But my cousin is powerful and persistent, and no amount of coercion was ever going to keep him from being his divine self. Me, on the other hand, definitely needed our grandmother's strict guidance. It's how I got my scholarship and changed my life for good.

"*You're interested in Isla Wright?*" Darren balks, his eyes going straight to Theo's.

"As in Ash's sister and Tanner's cousin?" Theo adds.

"That's the one," I say, noticing the way Theo takes a breath and sits back against his chair.

"How many of these people are there?" he asks, and Darren nods along.

"Right? And how is it they're managing to hook up with every single person we know?"

"I think that's a bit of an exaggeration," I say, chuckling as I take a mouthful of food. But I understand what he means. Supposedly there's six degrees of separation between almost everyone on the planet. But with Darren and the Wright family it probably feels like there's no separation at all.

"How did you even meet her?" Darren asks.

"She came into the bar with Ash when he was in town seeing Tahlia."

"I see. So she's the reason you didn't make it to my show?"

"Yeah," I say as I finish chewing. "I was with her."

"And now he's pussy whipped," Theo points out, to which Darren laughs.

"I'm so glad I never touch those things. They sound so dangerous."

"Right?" Theo agrees. "One good fuck and you're sucked right in."

"It's not like that," I say, finding their summation amusing. "It's her. There's something about her that's... different to everyone else. I crave her, but I have no idea how to win her."

"Uh oh," Darren says for the second time this visit. "That's not a problem you've encountered before.

"I'm aware. Which is what's got me so off balance. It's normally not this hard to get a date with someone."

"Well, you got *one*," Theo points out. "How did that come about?"

"It just happened." I shrug. "She came to the bar, thinking we were meeting there before the show, so we had a drink, got talking and then…"

"One thing led to another and now you're her snatch-slave for all eternity," Darren teases, making me almost choke on the mouthful of coffee I just took.

"This isn't helping, guys. I'm actually at a loss of what to do here. I mean, normally when I like a woman, I can shower her with attention—flowers, dinner, gifts—and it's cruisey. But with Isla…the woman's a Wright. That family has more money than God. So what can I, a wealthy bar owner, give her that she can't already give herself?"

"Dick, for one thing," Darren says as a matter of fact.

"I'm trying to be serious here, cousin."

"So was I," Darren says, somewhat indignant. Which is when the stoic Theo tilts his head to the side and shrugs.

"What about loyalty?" he starts. "I'll bet that's something she doesn't have a lot of in her life."

"Yesssss," Darren says as if it's almost a hiss. "That's precisely what all of them are lacking. That family is full of nothing but snakes. It's why Tanner and Ash bailed on their inheritance and made lives of their own. So if Isla is still caught up in the Wright Media machine, loyalty will literally be the one thing she's never had."

Sipping on my coffee, I give their insight a good amount of thought before I respond. "So, what you're saying is that I just have to be there for her? I have to keep showing up, and never giving up and eventually she'll see I'm the real deal."

Theo and Darren exchange a look before they turn back to me and nod. "As long as she's as interested in you as you are in her, it'll be the one thing that can prove to her you're not just another guy trying to raise his status in life by dating her."

"I'd never do that," I say, finding the idea of making something off someone else's back distasteful.

"We know that," Theo says. "But we're not the ones you've gotta convince."

ISLA

The sun bathes my face in its warmth the moment I step out of my apartment building. And for a moment, I wish I owned a dog so I could take it to Central Park and toss a ball with it for hours, just forgetting the weight of the world and reveling in the simplicity of each other's company for a bit. But that notion quickly dissipates when my phone chimes with about half a dozen reminders about meetings and report deadlines that demand my attention instead.

"Ugh," I grunt, shoving my cell back into my coat pocket as I make my way to the waiting car.

"How about we walk instead?" the smooth voice that enjoys filling my dreams says to my left, causing me to whip around and almost collide with the man. Luckily, Banks is more aware of his surroundings than I am and quickly pulls his arms aside, thereby saving the two takeaway coffees he's holding along with my cream peacoat.

"Good lord. Announce yourself to a girl next time?"

He grins. I melt. "Next time?"

"No. Not next time like I want you to keep showing up unexpected," I blabber, feeling the heat rise in my cheeks as my tongue feels too thick in my mouth. "But next time, as in the next time you start talking to a woman when she doesn't know you're there. It's a PSA from all women to you."

He's still grinning.

I'm still melting.

"I see. But that doesn't answer my question."

"You had a question?" I ask, my eyes fluttering as I try to adjust to his presence. I'm finding it harder and harder to do the thinking and paying attention thing whenever Banks enters my realm of existence.

"I asked if you'd like to walk with me to work this morning."

"Oh. Um. Wouldn't it take a good hour to walk to your work? I really don't have time for that."

Banks chuckles and shakes his head. "I live above the bar if you'll recall. I have no reason to be on the Upper East Side this early in the morning other than to walk to *your* work with *you*. I guesstimate that'll be about fifteen minutes if we hustle, twenty or more if we take our time."

"You're likely to make me late, Mr. Banks."

"Ah, but I bought you this amazing cappuccino and the pleasure of my conversational skills to make it worth your while."

Pressing my lips together I look from Banks to the car, knowing which of the two is the smart choice, and which one is purely self-indulgent, if not a bit misleading.

I suck in a breath. "I really don't want to accept and give you the wrong idea here," I say finally. As attracted to him as I am, and as much as I'm flattered that he sees fit to continue pursuing me, I can't in good conscience lead him on.

"I assure you, Isla, I am under no illusions here. You have made your position clear. You're not interested in a relationship. But I like you, and I'm fairly certain you like me. So at the very least, I figure we can manage friendship. Especially since your brother is dating my cousin's best friend and we're likely to run into each other in the future."

"Friends, you say?" I scrutinize him with a narrowed eye.

He grins and holds cappuccino out to me. "Friends who enjoy a good coffee and walks to work on sunny days."

"OK," I say, wrapping my hand around the warm cardboard cup. "We can be friends."

"OK," he repeats, looking over my shoulder and

saluting my driver with an, "I've got it from here, champ."

I chuckle at this man's eagerness to spend time with me, baffled even why a stunning entrepreneur with the world at his fingertips would bother himself with a woman from old money, old technology, and even older ideologies that most of the world couldn't even fathom being part of. Generationally, my cousins and I all hate the patriarchy that is Wright Media. But with Tanner and Ash out of the company, it's my two remaining cousins and I who are set to step up when our three fathers retire. Maybe then things can change. Maybe then, Wright Media can use its power for good instead of the attainment of more wealth and the willful enablement of ignorance.

But maybe that's a pipe dream.

"You seem very deep in thought," Banks says as we finish crossing the street and head toward East 79th Street. We've been making small talk about how business has been at his bar, along with how heavy my workload has been lately with a few tidbits about my family and his thrown in to round it out. He and his cousin, Darren, seem quite close.

"I was just thinking that it's been so long since I've walked to work. I'm so used to walking out of the door and getting straight into a waiting car that I fear I've grown spoiled."

"Heels hurting you already?" he asks, nodding toward my red-bottomed shoes.

"No." I laugh. "I was probably born able to walk in these without effort—something about breeding, my mother would have said—so it's definitely not the heels. It's more that I forget how close I live to everything. I really should do this more often."

"Deal," Banks says immediately.

"Deal?"

"Yeah. If the sun is shining. I'll be right out your door waiting to walk with you to work. It'll be our thing."

My heart stutters with longing and wanting, along with a warning. *Don't fall for beautiful men and promises, Isla.*

"Whether it becomes 'our thing' or not is something only time can tell," I say, stopping outside the entry to my building. "But I will say thank you for the coffee and the company this morning. It was definitely a nice change."

"My pleasure, Isla," he says with a nod and a smile, before he steps back and walks off the other way without so much as turning back.

Ugh. Why do I miss him already?

ISLA

A month later and Banks is true to his word. He keeps showing up with a coffee in hand and a smile on his face every morning when the sun shines, and sometimes even when it's not. It's getting to the point where I feel sad when I wake up to gloomy skies, which kind of sucks for me, because lying in bed and watching the rain streaking down my window used to be one of my favorite things to do. Now, it seems my favorite thing is walking to work with Banks.

"OK, so I think we've covered all the typical getting to know you conversations," Banks says as we take a slight detour since the morning air is particularly balmy today and I don't quite feel like fronting up to work just yet. "I've learned that you're close with your brother, but not with any of your other family members. That your best friend is also your personal assistant. That you prefer a night in over a night out. And that your favorite food is Chinese takeout." In turn, I've learned that he was raised by his grandmother, along with his cousin, throughout his teen years, after having been branded a troublemaker by his immediate family who didn't feel they could keep him on the straight and narrow anymore. His grandmother was a harsh woman, but her strict rules meant he was unable to fall into the kind of friendships that would lead him astray. He focused on his schoolwork, got himself a scholarship and then went to work on Wall St with his best friend, Ronan. While successful in his profession, he wasn't content, so he cashed out and decided to put all of his savings into setting up the bar. It was a huge gamble for him, but it paid off and he's been riding that high ever since. Oh, and his favorite food is Italian.

"Correct," I say. "Although you'll never catch me saying no to a nice apricot danish with just the right amount of custard and almond flakes on it."

"That's very specific," he says as he drops his empty coffee cup in the trash. "You see somewhere selling them?"

"Sure do. That little place over there. Handcraft. I like to stop for breakfast here when I'm avoiding going into the office."

"You do that a lot?" We continue talking as we cross the road and head for the busy café.

"Not really. Just when I've been working a lot of late nights and I just really want the chance to spend some time outside the same four walls. I didn't inherit my father's workaholic tendencies."

"You don't talk about him much."

"That's because there isn't much to say. He wanted his legacy to be his son's, and Ash didn't want that, so it fell to me. And try as I might, I don't think I could ever measure up."

"Is that something he said to you?"

We step inside and join the line. "Not in so many words. But it doesn't take a genius to work out when your voice isn't worth much. It's why I'm in the PR department instead of wheeling and dealing with my cousins, father and uncles upstairs. As a member of the board, I have to sign off on a lot of things, but I'm never included in the decision-making process."

"That seems a little unfair. Why do you continue working there if they treat you that way?"

I shrug. "Because it's what I know. Because I get paid way more than my job is worth. Because it's expected…"

"You know, I didn't grow up with a lot of expectation," he says, stepping forward as we get closer to the front of the line. "Keeping out of trouble was probably the biggest hope my mother had for me. So the pressure I put on myself to achieve was all my own. So, as my next getting to know you question, what would you have studied if you were to choose your path?"

We stop when we get to the front of the line and Banks orders two apricot danishes. But I tap my card before he can, insisting I pay. Then we leave the café with danishes in hands, smiles on our faces and a question still unanswered.

"Art," I say just before I bite into the sweet flaky pastry.

Banks looks at me in surprise. "Art?"

"Yeah. I have a real thing for giant puzzles that depict beautiful paintings. I'd love to be an artist and create something to put on them. But it doesn't even have to be art on puzzles. It could be art on the cover of notebooks, gift cards…even placemats. The possibilities are endless. And I think it would just be a really nice existence, you know? Sitting in a room with dappled sunlight coming in through the curtain, surrounded by paints and canvases. I could be happy like that." I take a massive bite of my danish and savor the sweetness along with the cozy feeling my words just gave me.

I'm so caught up in my own fantasy that I don't realize Banks still hasn't said anything. But when I look at him to make sure he didn't keel over from being bored to death, I find him looking right back at me with a bemused smile. "Then why don't you do that?"

I almost choke on a pastry flake. "Quit my job and

become an artist?" I shake my head. "That isn't...No. I can't. Especially not when I know that if I just hang in there a little longer, I'll be in the driver's seat of my career again. Dad is turning eighty soon, and his brothers—my uncles—are talking more and more about finally handing the company over to the next generation of Wrights. If I walk away now, I miss out on being the first woman with a controlling interest in Wright Media. I want to be part of the change instead of just blindly allowing the old ways to continue because I couldn't hack it anymore."

Banks stops walking in the middle of the busy sidewalk and catches me by the arm so I stop alongside him. Then he just places his hands on either side of my face and leans in to kiss me. I'm caught between surprise and acceptance as the sweet honey and butteriness of the danishes we just ate fill my senses completely as his tongue meets mine and moves in a soft caress. I can't help but let him completely take over as the world falls away around us. The hustle and bustle of the city disappears along with the jostling of pedestrians who are forced to walk around us, and all there is is us. His mouth on mine. His tongue gliding next to mine. His scent. His heat. *How have I managed to make it an entire month without falling into him again?*

"That wasn't very friendly," I whisper, almost completely out of breath as we pull apart and the city bursts back into my periphery again.

Banks smiles. "It wasn't meant to be."

I suck in a sharp intake of breath, knocked off balance as he slides one hand down to mine and entwines our fingers, starting to walk again like stopping me and kissing me during a conversation is commonplace for us.

"Wh-why did you do that?" I ask, stupidly just walking along holding hands with him.

"Because you have more substance than any woman I've ever known before and am likely to know going forward. I also did it because I don't just want to be your friend anymore." We stop in front of my building and he releases my hand, again turning to face me. "Have dinner with me."

I press my lips together and look up into his dark and inviting eyes. During these morning walks, I've come to really enjoy his company. But compared to the passion of that first night we spent together, this is all very benign. I like benign. Banks strikes me as a man who enjoys a little pizazz. Most men in suit vests and tailored shirts do. "I'm not an exciting person, Banks. I don't club. I don't even travel much. I'm just…I'm me."

"You seem plenty exciting to me."

"No. I'm serious here. When I said I like puzzles, I genuinely meant that that's like, one of my favorite things to do."

"OK," he says, completely nonplussed. "Then let's do a puzzle together. I'll bring the Chinese takeout."

Pulling my lips between my teeth, I try to swallow down the nervous feeling in my belly and force back the walls of protection in my mind that are acting like a little angel sitting on my shoulder reminding me of all the ways I've been hurt by charming men before.

"I don't know," I say, a memory of puzzle pieces flying across the room and hitting the wall surfacing despite my warring to hold it back.

"Then how about I promise not to kiss you even once? Unless of course you ask me to."

A smile pulls at my lips and I roll my eyes slightly, loving the smooth calm that emanates out of his voice. "I guess I can handle that."

"Yeah?"

"Yeah."

"OK. Then it'll be a dinner between friends. And to sweeten the deal, I'll also bring something I enjoy that most people I know find hideously boring."

"It's a deal," I say, grinning wide now as I hold my hand out to shake his, instead, having him take my hand and lift it to his lips, pressing a kiss against my upturned knuckles.

"It's a *date*," he drawls, releasing my still-warm hand, tingling from his lips and his touch. *Lawd my nipples are hard right now too!*

Thank god for padded bras.

"I thought you stipulated no kissing."

A grin lifts one side of his mouth. "That was during

our date. I never once said I wouldn't randomly kiss you while we walk."

Laughing, I shake my head in amusement as he steps back then wishes me a good day like he does every morning, leaving me feeling that against my better judgement, I'm still falling for him.

BANKS

When Friday arrives, I spend it keeping myself busy so I don't sit around watching the clock tick all day long. I throw myself into paperwork and preparations for the bar since I won't be there. And by the time I've run out of things to do—I even applied leather conditioner to my couch—I decide it's time to go and annoy my cousin. He has an innate ability to make time fly, and I really need that right now.

"Banksy, Banksy, Banksy," Darren says, stepping out the glittery door that marks the entry of the drag club he emcees and performs at, Queen's Delight.

"Darren, Darren, Darren," I reply, falling into step beside him as he waves his long red manicured fingers, indicating I need to follow him. "We going somewhere?"

"I need thread. My dress for tonight has a tear in it and I need the right color or it will be too obvious. So, off to the haberdashery store we go."

"OK. I'm up for an adventure."

Darren laughs. "There is no adventure here, sir. Just dire need. A queen must always look her best."

I nod down toward his feet as they clip clop against the sidewalk. "Those spiked-heel boots definitely accomplish that mission statement."

He manages a little skip of sorts as he lifts one foot to admire himself. "Yes, well, you kind of have to live what you sell."

"True words."

"So, my incredibly handsome, disappointedly straight cousin, what brings you my way on this fine afternoon?"

"I can't spend time with my favorite relative without having an ulterior motive?"

Darren stops walking and pushes his way inside a tiny hole in the wall store, practically overflowing with rolls of fabric. I have to turn sideways to make it past the aisle as I follow Darren to the wall displaying every possible color of thread you can imagine.

"You don't really need an ulterior motive," he says as he picks up two different shades of red and compares them to a tiny bit of thread he pulls from his pocket. "But this is certainly unusual. Is something going on?" He lifts his gaze from what he is doing and meets mine. "How's your pursuit of the unattainable woman going?"

"Well, I took yours and Theo's advice to be the guy she needs."

"A loyal one," Darren puts in as he returns one of the spools of red thread then gestures for me to turn so we can fight our way to the checkout counter.

"Not that I could be anything but. I'm not the kind of guy to tell you one thing then turn around and do another."

"And that's something I've always liked about you." He hands the cotton to the cashier then reaches in his pocket, freezing suddenly. "Dang. I forgot my wallet."

"I've got it," I say, pulling mine out and handing over the cash. He thanks me then we push back out onto the street, heading back toward the club. "So, I've been meeting her each morning and walking her to work."

"Romantic," he says, giving me an impressed nod.

"I figured it shows her that my interest isn't fleeting, nor is it dependent upon sex. And I'd hope she knows I'm not interested in her money."

"I think it's obvious you have your own. She could google you and find your net worth anyway."

"Do people actually do that?"

"They sure do."

"That feels a little dirty."

Darren shrugs. "Welcome to the human race."

I chuckle slightly, knowing he's right, but also knowing that the majority of people in this world are good at heart. I have fallen down many times in my life, and more often than not, someone who didn't need to helped me along the way.

"OK. So tell me how loyally bringing her coffee every morning and walking her to work is going for you?" he asks, getting us back on track.

"We have a date tonight," I say, nervousness blooming in my guts the moment I say it out loud.

Darren turns to me and smiles. "Ah-ha! Now I know why you're here. You want more dating advice. Theo and I are starting to call ourselves the fairy-gay-mothers since every straight person connected to us seems to think we have the magic answer to all things relationships and commitment."

"Don't you though?" I say with a smile, nudging him with my elbow as we arrive out the front of the Queen's Delight.

Darren laughs and places his hand on the silver door handle. "Seems that way. So, what's your question?"

"I honestly don't have one. I was coming to you to help fill my day if I'm honest. I've kind of done everything on my to-do list and I found myself at a loss until it's time to get ready and go."

"You're nervous." Darren reaches out and brushes a speck of dust off the front of my shirt. "Well, if it's any consolation, I don't think you have anything to be nervous about. You, sir, are a catch. Just ask any of the girls on the other side of this door. They would date you in a heartbeat. Every time they see me with you, they curse the gay gods for not making you one of us."

"All that does is tell me that I'm attractive to gay men," I say as I slide my hands into my pockets. "Wrong demographic."

"Oh no, we are the right demographic. We have better taste than all y'all put together. It's why you keep making us your best friends."

"Duly noted."

"Anyway, what is this date you're taking her on? Tell me how you're going to romance her."

"Dinner at her place."

"She's cooking for you?" His brow lifts like he thinks this night shows lots of promise.

"She doesn't like to cook."

"Oh. So you're cooking for her?"

"Not exactly. I'm bringing takeout."

"OK. So this is a Netflix and chill situation?"

"It's a Chinese and puzzle situation."

"Is that slang for some weird sex thing I don't know about?"

"No," I say with a laugh. "It's exactly what it is. I'm bringing the takeout and we're going to eat it while we do a puzzle."

"Oh god." Darren's manicured hand lands on his

chest, his face horrified. "Next you'll be telling me you've taken up knitting together."

"Well..." I start, just as Darren holds his hand up and turns his head to the side dramatically.

"Please don't. I couldn't take the boredom."

"I kind of think that's the point," I say, causing Darren to lower his hand and look back at me.

"What do you mean?"

"I think she wants me to want to stay through the boredom. I think it's the only way I'm going to earn her trust."

"Well, the woman has had not one, but *two* messy divorces. Her family tried to keep it out of the press as much as possible, but some of their rivals made her out to be a diva no man could handle."

"Yeah. I saw the articles. But after meeting her, I know that can't be further from the truth."

"The media rarely tells us the reality of a story. What is it Denzel said? That these days, it's not about truth or being right, it's about being first. It's about being entertaining and sensational for the sake of ratings and readership. And people like Isla, and Tanner and even Ash, end up getting caught in the crossfires of something that started even before they were born."

"I asked her why she keeps working there. You know, since everything we learn about Wright Media seems like it's run by the scum of the earth. And she said it's because she'll be the first woman with controlling power when her father steps down. She wants to stick it out and be part of the change."

"Oh, bless her. Does she realize those old men are going to sit on those thrones of theirs until they've turned to dust? And even then, I have a feeling they'll have holograms set up to keep up the illusion of never-ending power."

I chuckle a little at that visual. "It wouldn't surprise me. But no, I don't think she's realized that. She's just hanging on in there with her other two cousins, waiting for their chance to make things better."

"Well, I admire her tenacity. Just like I'm sure she'll come to admire yours."

I grin and check my watch, smiling when I see that if I head back home now, I'll have just enough time to shower, pick up the food and head over to the Upper East Side. Mission complete.

"You want to come in and say hi to the girls, or you on your way now?" Darren asks as he pushes the door open and a Tina Turner classic floats out and mixes with the sounds of the street.

"No, ma'am. I've got me a date to get ready for."

"Well, good luck. And don't do anything I wouldn't do—which really isn't much, so you pretty much have carte blanche on everything." He gives me a wink and I laugh.

"Thanks for the talk. Good luck with your show tonight too."

"Oh, cousin. I don't need luck. This place, it's where I was born to be. It's the only place on this planet I get to be me. Unapologetically."

When we part ways, I walk away ruminating over his final words, wondering if that's what I've found in Isla as well—a place to be unapologetically me. She may be thinking her favorite thing to do is mind numbingly boring to most, but she hasn't gotten a load of what I enjoy doing to entertain myself. It's not something I've shared with a single other person on this earth, and I have a feeling it'll either be the thing that brings us closer together, or the thing that'll make her realize I'm not the kind of man she thinks I am at all...

ISLA

"Let him up." My heart jumps into my throat as I give the word to the concierge, Carl, to allow Banks to come up to my apartment. A hand floats up to check my hair before it smooths down my clothes and my gaze falls to my socked feet, suddenly wondering if my choice to go with my normal puzzle and takeout attire was a good choice. After all, this is *technically* a date. An oversized sweater and thick woolen socks might be seen as total disinterest.

Wait. Do I want him to think I'm interested in him?

I turn and look into the entryway's mirror, taking in the messy bun, my gold-framed glasses—I normally wear contacts during the day but prefer my glasses at home—and the cream sweater that covers my body to the center of my thick yoga-pant-wearing thighs and cable knitted cream socks. If I was still in my early twenties, I could be considered adorable. But now that I'm pushing thirty, I'm starting to think I look like I've given up on life. Something I definitely haven't done.

Given up on love? Now, that's a completely different question and something I can unequivocally say yes to. But then a man like Banks comes along, rocks your world, buys you coffee then kisses you in the street, and suddenly you start wondering about all kinds of possibilities. So to answer my original question...yes, I do want Banks to think I'm interested in him. Question is, will he still be interested in me after spending an evening one step away from being bingo night at an aged care center?

Knock, knock, knock.

My breath catches in my throat as I turn away from the mirror and approach the front door, going a little too fast and sliding into solid wood with a thud when my socks fail to provide the friction I need on the slate flooring. *Oof.*

"Everything OK in there?" Banks's voice says from the other side.

"Ah. Yeah. Door's just a little stuck." I make a show of wrenching the door open. Then I'm just dumbstruck. Because Banks in a tailored pants and vest is stunning enough, but Banks in a pair of jeans, a T-shirt and bomber jacket *holding* a bag of Chinese food is what dreams are made of. "Ahhhhh."

Banks grins—like *that* could possibly help this situation. "Can I come in?"

"Oh. Uh. Yeah. Sure." I shake off the hungry, lusty images flashing through my mind as I step back, gesturing for him to come on in. "Wine?"

"Sure."

He follows me into the kitchen, lit by just the overhead light from the range hood as I pull two glasses out of my dark wooden cabinets and take a bottle of Sauvignon Blanc out of the fridge.

"Wanna grab a couple of plates from in here," I say, tapping the cupboard they're in with my foot. "The puzzle is this way."

Banks grins again, his eyes shining like everything about this evening is thoroughly entertaining for him. Then he gets the plates and follows me into the main living area.

"I normally just sit on the floor—the rug is really thick. But we can use the couch if you like. Pull the coffee table nice and close."

"The floor is fine," Banks says, taking a pack off his back I didn't notice at first and setting it on the floor to the side of the couch.

"Is that your contribution to the evening?" I ask, suddenly really wanting to know what's in his bag.

"It is. But I think that maybe we should do the puzzle first. My hobby isn't for everyone."

"Now I'm really intrigued."

"As you should be." He waggles his brows up and down then gets to work pulling boxes of delicious-smelling food out of a paper bag. "But that big reveal will have to wait until after we've eaten, *and* until after we've puzzled ourselves out."

"You think a puzzle lover can be 'puzzled out'?" I ask, taking the brand new thousand-piece box from beneath the coffee table and setting it on top.

"Not on a tiny thing like that," he says with a grin, his eyes falling to the box in my hands.

"I didn't want to overwhelm you on your first time," I say, batting my lashes and realizing that I'm flirting with him. Over puzzles. *Maybe this guy could be something more than a friend?*

"Don't go easy on me," he murmurs, the intimacy in his voice causing my insides to liquefy. "I can take it."

"OK. But remember you asked for it."

"With you, I'll always be asking for it."

With my cheeks heating, I slide the box back in place before pulling out a three-thousand piece one instead. "This is not only bigger, but it's also made of entirely black and white striped pieces. So it's almost impossible to guess where each piece goes."

I set it on top of the coffee table and Banks leans forward, nodding slowly as he peruses the box. "OK. Now, *this* is a challenge."

"Then we better get started." Picking up a set of

wooded chopsticks, I separate them with a snap and smile. I may have wanted this as a way to show Banks how unexciting my life really is, but now that he's here and so willing, I think this night may prove to be the best date I've ever been on.

BANKS

"What are your feelings toward ice cream?" I ask, standing up from my position on the floor and stretching out my back. Isla was right when she said the rug was comfortable, and her couch provided just the right amount of back support to keep me wanting to keep my butt planted while we chatted, ate and worked on that impossible puzzle together. We're two hours in, and barely one quarter through.

"Ice cream and I are great friends. I'm a big fan of mint choc-chip."

I nod slightly, conceding that her flavor choice is gold standard. "On its own, or with a scoop of chocolate fudge to add a little punch?"

She grins. "Add in a strong coffee to that and you've got yourself a dessert buddy," she says, holding out her hand and letting me help her to her feet.

Wrapping my big hand around hers, I help her up, adding a gentle tug at the end so she has no choice but to brace herself against my chest. *God it feels good to have her this close.*

"You did that on purpose," she says, smiling up at me, her voice a little huskier than it was a moment ago.

"I'd be lying if I said I didn't."

"You promised no funny business."

"I promised no kissing. There's a lot we can do without kissing, Isla."

Her body shudders in response and I feel each and every tiny tremor. "I'm sure there's plenty. But that's not what we're here for, is it?"

"I don't know, Isla. What exactly are we here for? I mean, besides you trying your best to convince me that my interest in you is completely misplaced."

"It is." She pushes back through her hand and steps away from me.

"Don't you think I get to decide that?"

"Yes, actually. I do. Which is why I'm letting you know who I am—who the real me is—before you build up some fantasy of the rich heiress and her yachts and connections. Some men seem to think that being with me is an easy ticket to the high life. But all that stuff you see wealthy people doing on TV and in magazines isn't my style. I like being right here in my apartment. I like eating the same food, doing the same activities, and I don't think you understand how...simple I really am."

"And I don't think you understand that simple is exactly what I want. I don't know what pre-conceived notions you have about me, but I don't want nor do I need your money or your connections. I have plenty of my own, and frankly, I'm insulted you'd even *suggest* that's what I was doing with you." I lean over and grab my backpack, releasing a sigh as I do. "I came here tonight thinking, yes! Finally! Finally she's getting it. Finally she understands that I'm interested in *her*. Not your name, not the people you can influence with it. Just you. If I wanted a yacht or a ticket to the high life, I could get it myself—the same as I have with everything else in my life. I'm not a man who preys upon the success of others to lift myself up. I'm a man who creates my own opportunities. I'm a man who works for what I want. And I'm a man who persists when others wouldn't. I get that you've been hurt before, Isla. The kinds of walls you've got built up don't come from living a fairy-tale life. But I also know that I don't deserve to pay for the shitty behavior of others." I sling my backpack on my shoulder and turn to walk out. "I'll see you round, Isla."

I get about two steps away before her voice stops me. "Wait."

Stopping, I turn and face her with raised brows. "Why?"

"Because..." She rolls her lips together, and fuck me if I don't want to rush right over there and suck them free before laving every inch of her body with my tongue. I fucking ache for this woman.

"Because why?"

"Because you haven't shown me what's in your backpack yet."

A smile bursts to life on my face and I swipe a hand over my mouth, slipping the pack of my shoulder with the other. "Showing you this makes me vulnerable, Isla."

"I know you don't think it, Banks. But I feel really vulnerable here too. I don't..." Her eyes stray to the unfinished puzzle on the table. "I don't share this with anyone either."

"What about your ex-husbands?"

She barks out a laugh. "The last thing either of them wanted was to spend a night in eating takeout and doing puzzles. They were all about the show. They both wanted to be seen, and I quickly learned that my substance lied in being an arm ornament and a bank card. You'd have thought I learned the first time, right?"

"We all want to trust that the people we love, love us the same way we love them."

She sniffs slightly as she nods, fighting against her emotions. "I might have a few trust issues."

"OK," I say, my voice whisper soft. "Then maybe we work through those one at time. Together."

"I'd like that," she whispers.

"Guess I should show you my weird hobby then, huh?"

"Is it D&D?" she asks, her hands fisted at her mouth in anticipation.

"No." I laugh, unzipping the backpack and reaching in. "It's weirder."

A gasp escapes her mouth as I pull out the bamboo hoop securing a piece of cloth with the faded image of a dragon printed on it and colorful threads stitched over most of the print, bringing it to vibrant life. "You cross stitch?"

"Yeah." I'm thankful for the pigment of my skin's ability to hide the deep flush of embarrassment that reaches up my neck and makes me wish for a bucket of ice. It takes everything I have not to shove that hoop back into my bag and away from her inquisitive gaze

"Can I touch it?" she asks when she moves closer to get a better look.

My hand shakes. "Sure."

With a slow lift of her hand, she runs the tips of her fingers over each careful stitch I've made, moving from the fire coming out of the dragon's mouth, all the way to the tail then down to the unfinished claws. "What do you do with them when you're finished?"

I bounce a shoulder. "Nothing. I put them in a box and store them all in a cupboard."

"I'd frame them and put them on my wall."

"There'd be no space on your walls if you framed every one I've completed."

"You've done that many?" Her eyes lift to mine, and in an instant, the nervous vulnerability I was feeling completely dissipates, because in her eyes is nothing but wonder. She seems to actually think this is cool. *I knew I was falling for her for a reason.*

"Yeah," I whisper, my eyes dropping to her lips because all I want to do right now is kiss her and make passionate love with her the way we did that first night. Except this time, neither of us would be leaving. We'll be waking up next to each other so I can eat her for breakfast.

"Banks."

My eyes snap to hers as I swallow my urges deep down.

"I think I want you to kiss me now."

I slide the cross stitch back into my bag and set it aside. "You think?"

"I know," she whispers, licking her lips with her perfect pink tongue. "It feels like we see each other clearly now."

I grin as I slide my hand against the curve of her neck and brush my thumb against the underside of her cheek. "And it turns out we're both nerds."

A smile brightens her face as laughs. "Will you teach me how to cross stitch?"

I lean in and brush my lips against hers. "Abso-fucking-lutely," I murmur, before kissing her with everything I have in me.

ISLA

Something about the way he kisses me knocks the air out of my lungs. Every. Single. Time.

I can hardly do it justice describing it, but when Banks's mouth is moving against mine, nothing in this world compares. Not puzzles. Not choc-mint ice cream. And definitely not takeout Chinese or a night alone, snuggled under a blanket watching Netflix until I fall asleep. Previous to meeting Banks those were all of my favorite things. But now—as much as I've denied myself the pleasure—being kissed by Banks is definitely at the top of that list.

My body aches for more, and I moan into his mouth from the pleasure of it.

"I want you, Isla," he murmurs, his hands wrapping around my waist before he hoists me onto the nearest surface, which happens to be the buffet I use to store all of my finished jigsaw puzzles. My back collides with the Tiffany blue wall as he pushes my legs apart with his knees and I make quick work of shoving his jacket from his shoulders. I need the heat of his skin. Now.

Tugging at the bottom of his shirt, I scrape my nails along his tender flesh, feeling the goosebumps develop as I glide my palms up to his ribs. "I want you too, Banks."

He moans, sucking on my lower lip before he releases it with a pop then lifts his arms, helping me get his tee the rest of the way off. Then we just pause for a moment, his head hovering near mine, my hands against the warmth of his chest, the rapid thudding of his heart beating out the only sound in the entire room along with our heavy breathing. We lock eyes, searching in each other for any sign of hesitation.

"Please." I wrap my hands around his ribs and urge him closer, moaning when his mouth collides with mine again, his fingers sliding beneath my sweater and skirting across the soft skin of my belly.

Everything inside me flutters, both with anticipation and nerves. The last time we did this, alcohol was involved. So I didn't pause to think about the size of my stomach, the stretch marks over my hips or the abundance of cellulite that covers my thighs. I am by no means a small woman and never have been. I'm tall and I'm solid, and I like junk food far more than I should and dislike exercise more than I have the right to. But I am me. And alone, there's never anyone to answer to. Never anyone to scrutinize my curves and question whether I should be wearing what I'm wearing or eating what I'm eating. Being naked around a man with a body as perfect as Banks's is...confronting.

"Maybe we should take this into the bedroom?" I whisper, shuddering as his fingers skirt along the hem of my yoga pants, causing my insides to tighten and throb.

"Soon," he whispers, his mouth moving to the curve of my neck and sucking gently. "I want to taste you right here first. We never got to that dessert."

I let out a moan as his tongue traces my pulse, but then I react by gripping his wrists when he goes to remove my sweater. "Wait."

"What's wrong?"

I shake my head. "Nothing. I just...It's very open in here."

"Are you worried someone will see?" He turns and looks over his shoulder like he's looking for someone else in the room. "Is there someone here I don't know about?"

"No. It's just that last time, we were drinking. And this time, well, you're about to get the real show in technicolor."

"And?"

"And I have stretch marks and cellulite and *rolls* of skin where you have abs and muscles."

He hooks a finger under my chin and forces me to look up at him while he places his other hand on the buffet beside me, his dark eyes boring into mine. "Do you honestly think I give a damn about any of that?"

"Maybe. I don't know enough about you yet."

"Well, considering I spent a single night with you then pursued you relentlessly for the chance at another, I think you can be pretty confident that I find you sexy as hell." He places his hands on my thighs and pulls me against him, the evidence of his desire pressing squarely into the center of my aching core. "I've thought about you endlessly since that night. I dream about the softness of your skin and long to taste and touch you, sink myself deep inside you." He moves to lift my sweater over my head again, and this time, when he makes it to my ribs, I let him, lifting my arms above my head then taking a deep breath as the cream fabric is pulled free of my hair, knocking my glasses off my face in the process.

"Oh shoot!" I grab for them, doing a little juggle before they clatter to the floor, but ultimately failing when they tumble to the ground with a clatter.

"Shit. That was supposed to be a really intense moment for us where I was totally focused on proving to you how sexy I find every inch of you," he says, squatting down and scooping them up.

When he stands and gently sets them back on my face and hooks them over my ears, I'm smiling up at him. "It was," I say, reaching up and running my hands over his well-defined chest again. "Your words and your actions were absolutely perfect."

"Yeah?" He smiles, leaning in and brushing his lips against mine. "Because I meant it all. I'm obscenely attracted to all of you." As he talks, he lowers to his knees, pressing soft kisses against the swell of my breasts, the curve of my belly, the faded stretch marks next to my belly button and then the angry-looking purple ones on my hips. "Every bit of skin. Every soft curve." He pressing my thighs a little wider and kisses me there too. "And every sweet-smelling valley. You're soaked for me, aren't you?"

"Yes."

A rumble of pleasure floats out of him, and when his eyes lift to mine, he hooks his fingers in the waist of my yoga pants then drags them down my legs, along with my underwear. Then I'm naked, save for my bra, and with the heat in his gaze and the way he licks his lips in anticipation of his next move, I completely forget what I was ever worried about when keeping this man out of my life and my bed. I obviously had rocks in my head.

"I ache for you, Isla," he murmurs, pressing a kiss at the place where my thighs meet my sex. I shake from wanting more. "Tell me you've been thinking about doing this again as much as I have."

"I have," I admit, knowing that anything else would

be a bold-faced lie. Ever since that night in his bed, I've dreamed of little else. It's like he ruined me for anyone and everything else. Even my vibrator is no match for the sexual stylings of Banks Johnson.

He lets out a moan, reaching up and palming my breast, his thumb brushing across my sensitive nipple at the same time as his tongue connects with my clit. "God, you taste good. Better than ice cream in my opinion."

I grin through my moan, leaning back as he buries his face between my thighs, his fingers tugging on my nipple as his tongue flicks and swirls around my sensitive bud. My hands grip the edge of the buffet's counter, while my body seems to writhe of its own accord, wanting more and more until I just can't take it anymore.

"Holy shit!" I call out. "Banks! Oh god!"

My head falls back and connects with the wall as my release takes over, weeks of pent-up frustration from denying myself this simple, perfect, yet oh-so-risky pleasure overwhelming me. I've known for a long time that I'm better off on my own, but there's no denying the connection Banks and I share. And now that I'm letting him in, I also know I can't go back to whatever we were before. Question is, how far can I let him in without compromising on the promises I've made to myself?

"Mmmm." Banks moans as his arms wrap around

my thighs and he flattens his tongue, lapping up my juices as he holds on tight, forcing me to continue to ride the waves of my orgasm until he's ready to bring me back down.

"Banks. Please. It's too much. I need you. I need you inside."

"God, you taste good." He lifts his head slightly, pressing a kiss then a long lick against my seam that causes my hips to jolt and for the both of us to laugh.

"Cheeky," I say, panting and smiling as he wipes over his face and pushes his jeans to the floor, cock in his hand as he rubs his tip through my juices.

"Desperate," he counters, pushing his thick shaft in as he brings his mouth to mine and fills me completely. "Home."

Something stutters in my chest at his words as his hips begin to roll and we clutch on to each other, the firm collision of our bodies causing emotions and need to flow through me in a frightening way. Yes. I have feelings for Banks. Turns out, I have a lot of feelings for Banks. But I had feelings before too, and I've gotten to the point where I just can't trust them. More than that, I can't trust myself.

But I want to trust Banks.

Winding my legs around his waist, I grind back as he thrusts, my mouth resting against his shoulder as his tucks his face into my shoulder, sucking on my skin with a laving of his tongue until the both of us almost pass out from the intensity of our crashing hips.

"Fuck," he groans, stilling with a final thrust as my walls pulse around him, squeezing out our combined orgasm as we pant and kiss and laugh because honestly, that was crazy intense. Some things you do are better the first time, but with Banks, that doesn't seem to be the case. I don't think I've ever been fucked quite so well. This could become an addiction if I'm not careful.

"Did you just give me a hicky?"

"Yeah," he says, tenderly kissing the skin on my shoulder with wet lips. "Got a little carried away."

I angle my head in a way that I can somewhat see the purple welt. "As long as it's under my clothes, and I don't have to explain it at the office on Monday, you can give me a love bite anywhere you like."

He quirks a brow. "Anywhere? Well, in that case." He hauls me off the buffet and starts walking out of the living room with me wrapped around him before pausing and turning side to side. "Wait. Where is your bedroom?"

"That way," I say, nodding to my right side before he sets off walking again.

"You might be sorry you gave me permission to do this, by the way," he says as we flop on the bed and he kisses me again, seeming just as hungry despite only finishing moments ago.

"I guess that's up to you, isn't it? Are you going to

give me something to be sorry about?" I ask, knowing it's a loaded question, but the nerves and the trepidation and…I've got issues is all I can say.

Banks pushes up on his arms and holds himself over me, taking a long moment to search my eyes before he replies. "Not if I can help it," he murmurs, before bringing his mouth to mine again.

ISLA

I'm not sure why, but for some reason when I head downstairs ready for work on Monday morning, I'm surprised to find Banks standing there, coffees in hand like always. I also don't miss the feeling of relief that hits me either.

"Hey," I say, smiling broader than I probably intend to as he passes me my coffee, made just the way I like it.

"Hey, yourself," he says as we start walking and his fingers catch mine. It's just a little hook off our middle and pointer fingers, like we're testing this out. Or more like he's testing me out. It's no secret that he's doing his best not to push me. But as was evident on Friday night when he almost walked out of my door, even a patient man like Banks has his limits. Time will tell if his limits and mine align. Because I can't promise to lower all my walls just because we get along and have mind-blowing sex. No. The only thing I can promise Banks Johnson is time. It's all I have to give right now.

"Why is it that you seem surprised I'm even here this morning?" he asks after a while of walking in quiet contemplation.

Swallowing the mouthful of coffee I've just taken, I bounce a shoulder. "I hoped that didn't translate into my expression. But obviously it did. I was definitely very happy though."

"Oh, I saw that too," he says, turning to me slightly and bumping me with his elbow. "And for the record, if that sun is shining and the weather is suitable for walking, then I will still be here. Unless of course I wake up in bed next to you. If that's the case, I'll still get you coffee, but I'll send you to work with a different kind of smile. And if it's raining that day, we'll take your car."

The promise in his voice makes me squirm, and I wonder if I now look like I applied too much blush this morning.

"Admittedly, I did have a different kind of smile on my face this morning," I say, a warm feeling spreading up my arm when he laces our fingers completely.

"Oh, really?" He waggles his brows up and down as he looks at me.

"Mind out of the gutter. I was talking about a certain hicky that spells out somebody's name. I feel like you've staked out a claim."

"I have."

"We'll see," I say, grinning to myself as we walk along, quietly drinking and just enjoying each other's company.

I can't deny the warmth pooling in my lower belly as I think about the hicky on my thigh that spells out 'Banks'. Ridiculous as it sounds, it's also crazy hot. Looking at it and remembering his mouth on my body produced a carnal desire in me that did nothing but urge me to want more from the man who keeps showing up at every turn.

And when I get to work after a sneaky kiss goodbye out the front of the building, Karen seems to sniff out the change in me the moment I walk past her desk on the way to my office.

"You've had *sex*," she declares under her breath as she follows me in, closing the door behind her with a thud.

"That is such an inappropriate thing for an assistant to say to her boss," I say as I drop my bag and take a seat behind my desk, powering up my computer.

She plops herself in the seat across from me and waves her hand dismissively. "We are constantly inappropriate around each other. So this is nothing. Tell me everything. I want details. Was it the dirty-talking guy who sent you flowers because they reminded him of the color of your lady lips?"

"You are so crass!" I cover my mouth and giggle,

unable to hide the flush in my face as I cross my legs and sit back.

"What is on your thigh?" she gasps, her eyes going wide as she shoots out of her chair and leans in close, making me realize the letter 's' is poking out from underneath my skirt.

"That is nothing," I say primly, uncrossing my legs and pulling my skirt down lower.

"Oh, no, girlfriend. That is definitely something." She moves around to my side of the desk, and since she's my best friend, I hitch my skirt up a little and let her see my special little brand. She gasps and covers her mouth, stepping back with her eyes alight. "I fucking love this guy for you. When am I going to meet him?"

"I don't know," I say, pulling my skirt back down again as she takes her seat. "Everything about us is so new, and I honestly don't feel ready to put any extra pressure on us. I need to take this slow."

"A love bite that spells his name is not taking something slow, dear girl," she says.

"I kind of disagree with that because we've had a whole month of getting to know each other outside of the sheets before we got back into them again."

She nods her head slowly as she listens. "I like it. You're making him work for it."

"It's not even that. I just don't want to repeat the mistakes of my past by rushing into something just because it feels good. I've done that twice already and both times it turned out that those men were not the men I thought they were in the beginning. I came out of both those marriages with even worse self-esteem than I had when I went in them and it's taken me a long time just being happy as me. I don't want to give that away again. I want to be cautious this time."

"OK. I get it. I mean, I wasn't around to witness the fallout of your first marriage. But I did know you during your second and I saw how much he broke you. So, I really do understand. However, I'm not here advocating that you marry the guy. Hell, I don't even believe in marriage after the shitshow I witnessed growing up. Andy actually proposed to me not long ago and it honestly almost broke us up."

"Are you serious? Why didn't you tell me about that?"

She bounces a shoulder. "Because we managed to sort it out rather quickly. He's the love of my life for crying out loud."

"Then why don't you want to marry him?"

"Because I don't need that to be happy with him. And after we talked, he realized that he only wanted it because he thought it was the logical next step. After I assured him that all I want is him, it stopped being an issue for us." She sits forward and looks me dead in the eyes. "Now, I'm not saying that you guys need to be super serious about each other off the bat. But I am saying that I hear you, and as your best friend I'm here to support you. Even if that means telling you that you're being an idiot occasionally."

"You think I'm being an idiot?"

"Well, yeah. Because you're putting the pressure of two broken marriages on a guy who seems to be willing to go out of his way to be with you. He's brought you coffee every morning and walked you to work, taking the time to learn as much as he can about you, and he even agreed to do a puzzle with you instead of going on a date—which was obviously an awesome idea because you look rather well fucked this morning."

"You've got me there."

"I know. I'm *very* perceptive, and as the perceptive one in our friendship, I'm also suggesting that you drop the idea of all relationships leading to marriage and a future right into the trash. No one needs that pressure. You and Banks can enjoy the absolute fuck out of each other and never commit to a single thing besides fucking and making time for each either. All relationships are based on friendship. And if you add passion to that, you've got something really special. So just be clear about your boundaries with him and enjoy it." She leans in close and smiles. "I dare you."

BANKS

"Shouldn't you be at work or something?" I ask Ronan as he sits on one side of the bar, drinking Grey Goose while I take inventory—something he's currently depleting on my dime.

"I should. But I just fired my assistant, and if I go back there, I'll fire the whole damn team too."

"Not the promotion you thought it'd be?" I ask, doing a quick count of the mixers in the cocktail fridge. It's late afternoon, and the only employees I have on site at the moment are my manager and the cleaners. Ronan is the one freeloader, and if he keeps drinking at the rate he is, he's going to be hammered before sundown.

"Nope." He pops his P as he drains his glass then crunches on a piece of ice. "I thought I'd have this unstoppable teams of analysts. But instead, I have a bunch of green kids who are too scared to make a single fucking call without running it by me first. It's painful. I'm just a glorified babysitter."

"And what made you fire your assistant?"

"I told her not to let any of them in my office and she did. So now she's gone."

"Harsh."

He shrugs. "Probably. I'm a cunt, aren't I?"

I shrug. "Probably."

Placing his hand on his face, he groans. "This was supposed to be career changing, man. If I can't get these guys investing like they know what they're doing, I'll end up making less than I was when I was on someone else's team."

"Then teach them how. Show them how to be the fearless investor you are. You've seen fucking Field of Dreams enough times to know that you have to build it before they come."

"Jesus. I swear that was the only video tape your grandmother owned."

"She watched that movie until the tape wore out. She was a big Kevin Costner fan and a hater of new technology. Took me ages to get her another working copy."

"She wouldn't switch to DVD?"

"No way. And now that there's internet and you can stream? She'd consider that the devil's playground. 'Not in my house,'" I mimic, causing Ronan to laugh just as my skin pricks and I lift my head, feeling her before I see her. "Hey there."

"You look surprised to see me," Isla says, walking toward me with that sultry sway of her hips that has me practically growling with a need to get her upstairs into my apartment.

Ronan lets out a low whistle. "Who is *this*?"

"This is Isla," I say by way of introduction. Isla smiles and pauses at the bar next to him. "Isla, this is Ronan."

"Oh!" She says immediately, holding out her hand. "The guy you grew up with."

"That'd be me," he says, nodding as he shakes her hand in return. "And you're the unobtainable woman obtained."

I wince before taking the bottle of vodka away from him. "That'll be enough for you," I say, shaking my head because the asshole is going to scare her away before we've even worked out what we are to each other. Luckily, Isla just laughs.

"Oh, I'm still unobtainable," she says.

Ronan gives me a look that's a mix between being disappointed the bottle is gone and thinking I've gotten myself in over my head with this one. And maybe I have.

During the years of our friendship, neither of us could be what you'd call a long-term kind of guy. We've both been one-hundred percent career and goal driven.

But where he and I differ now is that I've achieved all my career goals, and now I want something more. And I want that something with Isla. I don't care if I have to work every day to get it, I'm willing to put in the time until she's sure I'll never walk away from her. Which I won't, because after all, I did put my name on her. She's mine now.

"Sounds like you've got a battle on your hands, buddy," Ronan says, reaching into his pocket and pulling out his wallet. "Guess I should leave you two to it." He goes to put money on the counter to cover his drinks, but I wave him away—we do this dance all the time, but pride says he at least needs to offer. "Nice to meet you, Isla. Hopefully this guy treats you well enough that we meet again." He takes her hand and presses a light kiss to the back of it, causing a slight possessive flare to tighten my chest. But then he turns to me and gives me a salute, heading to the door with his hands in his pockets, whistling like he doesn't have a care in the world.

"I didn't mean to chase him away," she says once we're alone. "Your manager let me in, and I didn't realize you were entertaining."

I laugh as I close up the inventory folder and give her my full attention. "I wasn't entertaining. I was working. He was slacking off, and you came at the perfect time. In fact, any time is perfect where you're concerned."

"Such a sweet talker," she says, rolling her lips as she looks around the quiet space. "It's different in here when no one's around."

"Yeah. I kinda like it better this way if I'm honest, but I need the people in to pay the bills."

"I'll bet," she says, seeming a little nervous as she meets my eyes. "Is there…somewhere we could talk?"

Uh-oh.

"Ah, sure. Is everything OK?" I step out from behind the bar in gesture for her to move toward my office.

"Everything is fine," she assures me. "I was just thinking about things, and I realize that you and I haven't really set any ground rules."

We both step into my office and I press the door closed behind her, placing my hands on my hips because I'm pretty sure I want to be standing for this conversation. "Ground rules?"

"Yeah," she says, stepping a little closer to me. "For our… whatever this is."

I really want to call it a relationship, but I don't think that's what she wants to hear right now. "OK."

"I realize that none of this has been particularly normal so far, and I'm more than aware that it's my own hang ups over past relationships that's been the anchor stopping us from moving forward."

"OK?" I draw the last letter out, intrigued as to where this is going.

"I was wondering if maybe we could just take the word 'relationship' out of our vocabulary. I don't want to slow down or go back to how we were before this weekend, but if we can stop looking at this like it has to lead somewhere, then maybe it will take the pressure off."

I take a pause and think about her words, wondering what they mean for me and what I want from her. Is this something I can accept if it means I have the chance to be with her?

"What are you saying here?" I ask finally. "That you want to keep hanging out and fucking each other, but you don't want to put a label on it?"

She thinks for a moment then nods. "Yes. I think that's exactly what I want."

"So, what you're asking for is a friends with benefits situation?"

Her brow lifts like she hadn't actually considered it that way before she nods. "I suppose so. But with some rules."

"Rules." I step closer to her, feeling the heat of her body against mine when I stop. "What kind of rules?"

She licks her lips as she tilts her head up to meet my eyes, and I take the opportunity to back her against the door, deciding I want to have her any which way I can. She smiles when I cage her in. "Exclusivity."

"Agreed. I would lose my mind if the new toy I just

wrote my name on fell into the hands of someone less skilled."

"And modest too." She giggles as her hands lift to my chest and she fingers a button on my shirt.

"We all need to be aware of our talents, Isla. And yours is turning me the fuck on every time you move." I lean in, desperate to kiss her, but she places her fingers on my lips and stops me.

"We're discussing the rules."

"Hmm. Well, if we have to discuss things, we can at least make it fun," I say, sliding my hand down her side and dragging her skirt up her legs. Her breathing deepens but she doesn't object, and when my fingers slide into the side of her panties, her silken heat makes me groan. "Seems this is exactly what you wanted from me."

"I want a lot from you, actually. It's why I'm here." She gasps as I slide my fingers into her heat, massaging her tight walls as her breathing quickens and she clings to my biceps, her leg lifting to hook on my thigh and give me better access.

"Tell me more about this 'no relationship' deal."

"We get each other. No walls." She pauses to swallow as I slip my fingers in and out, using my thumb to apply pressure to her clit. "No finding reasons to stay away. We're together, but we're still ourselves—Oh god, that feels good."

"So you want all the passion and the benefits of a

relationship without losing who you are as an individual?"

"Yes," she gasps, her insides clenching around my fingers as her grip on my arms tightens. "Yes." She spasms against my hand, her clit pulsing along with her orgasm against my thumb as she gasps and nods, riding out her release. "Yes."

"OK," I say, dropping my mouth to hers and kissing her softly as I fuck her gently with my fingers, bringing her back down slowly from her high. "I can do that for you."

"Really?"

I pull my hand from between her legs and nod. "Yeah." I bring my hand to my mouth and lick her juices from my fingers with a pleasurable hum. "For a woman who tastes as good as you do, I think I'd do just about anything."

"I really appreciate that."

"And I appreciate your honesty, because I think I've made my unwavering interest in you very obvious."

"You have. And I know I've been playing my own cards close to my chest this past few weeks, but..." she says, sliding down the door until she's on her knees. "I think it's about time I get a taste of you too."

I brace my hands against the back of the door. *Sweet Jesus I'm in for a treat.*

ISLA

So far, being together without the pressure of a future has been amazing. We see each other a few times a week, spend Friday or Saturday nights together—depending on Banks's work schedule—then spend a lazy day in bed, doing puzzles at my place or cross stitch at his. And I have to say I'm getting quite good at this new hobby we're sharing. Banks even bought me a gold needle like his so it runs smoother through the cloth, leaving less of an imprint with each stitch. It's been lifechanging. Actually, being with Banks has been lifechanging. I have no idea what I was fighting against in the beginning.

"Do you think you'll ever want children?" he asks in the quiet of his room one Saturday night about two months into our new arrangement. *Oh, that's right. I was fighting against rushing into any commitment.*

"What makes you ask that?" I roll over to my side so I'm facing him, and he places his hand on my hip, moving his fingers soothingly against my skin.

"Well, we do spend a lot of time performing the act that creates them, so..." He bounces a shoulder and smiles, and even though I've been the recipient of his magnetic smiles for months now, it still makes my belly flip.

"We do," I say, placing my hand against his chest and playing with the tiny twirls of chest hair that dust across his steely pecs. "Which is why I have a birth control device fitted. That way we won't have any mishaps."

"You'd consider a kid we made a mishap?"

Lifting my eyes to his, I roll my lips together, nerves fluttering about in my chest now. It's not that I don't want children. Hell, if you could guarantee me a happy marriage that wouldn't end in divorce and turn that kid into a transient being who floats between two houses, getting constantly introduced to one parent's new girlfriends, while the other does little to veil the contempt she holds over her ex-husband's—your father's—philandering ways, then I'd be on board. But as the record stands, I've already proven my inability to maintain a healthy relationship with a spouse, so for the sake of everyone involved, I just don't think bringing a child into an uncertain situation is the greatest idea. It's not about me.

"An unintended pregnancy is definitely a mishap, but I would never call a child a mistake."

"But you don't want one?"

Pulling my hand back, I wiggle slightly on the bed, tucking them against my chest as I try to come up with an appropriate response. One that doesn't have me coming off as a heartless and selfish woman, because that's not where my intentions are. But that's not easy to articulate. Especially when you're a woman of a certain age and people start expecting you produce the next generation, like you're some sort of surname factory bred to strengthen the family name.

"It's not that I don't want to be a mother. I genuinely do. I just don't think it's fair to bring a child into an uncertain situation."

"You think I'd skimp on parenting duties?"

I shake my head. "No. I think you'd be a wonderful father. But as a daughter of divorce and a woman with two failed marriages in her past, I just don't want to put my own child through custody changes and loyalty tests and..." I let out a sigh. "I just think kids need stability, and I'm not willing to have one unless I can be sure I can provide that."

He studies me for a long time before he lets out his breath and nods. "OK," he says finally, before rolling on his back.

"OK?"

He turns his head to look at me. "Yeah. I'm saying that I get where you're coming from."

"Are you mad?"

He frowns. "Why would I be mad? I asked a question and you answered honestly."

"I suppose that depends on what your answer to that same question would be."

With his hand on his chest, I watch the rise and fall of his body as he looks up at the ceiling before turning back to me and answering. "I'd say yes."

"Does it change things for you that I didn't give you the same answer?"

"No," he says simply. "I think I'd be surprised if you did, considering your stance on relationships in general."

"Listen, I know that what I've asked of you is a lot. And if you don't think you can keep doing this with me, I'll understand." I lay my hand back on his chest, and he moves his hand to cover mine right away.

"I don't want this to end," he says, turning his whole body back toward me until he's holding himself on top of me while pushing my hands up over my head. "In fact, no matter what rules or restrictions you want to put on this, no matter what name you wanna call it, I'm in this one hundred percent, Isla. Nothing is going to change that."

Relief floods through me at the intensity of his words, quickly getting replaced with desire when his cock presses against my entrance and pushes slowly into my depths, making me moan and gasp with longing, even though we literally only just finished doing this less than half an hour ago. I just can't seem to get enough of him.

"Harder," I cry, my body aching with a need for more of him. "Harder."

He draws his hips back, driving in harder each time, my body shifting up his bed with each solid thrust. It feels so good, this slamming together of pelvises that seems to fill me so deeply I can feel his cock everywhere. Naturally, I want more of it.

"Harder!" I moan.

With an almighty thrust, he slams his hips into and sends my body directly into his wooden bedhead, my head hitting with such force that my body decides to respond by releasing some pressure at the other end.

That's correct, ladies and gentlemen. I just farted during sex. And if that's not embarrassing enough, I also came. *What the actual hell?*

Banks freezes, and my hands go to face to hide my mortification as I moan—both from mortification and the fact my orgasm is winding down. "Oh my god! I can't believe I just did that!"

There's a shaking sensation on the bed and when I peek through my fingers, Banks's entire body is rocking with laughter. And since his cock is still buried in me, it feels pretty good.

"This is not the time to be laughing, Banks!"

"Really?" he asks, shifting his balance to wipe a tear from his face. "Because if this isn't one of those times, I don't know what is."

"Oh, it's fine for you! You're not the one who just farted and came at the same time."

He bursts into a fresh bout of laughter, rolling off me and landing on his back, clutching his stomach because he's laughing so hard.

"You are so mean," I say, laughing a little myself now. "I am never going to eat before sex again."

"Oh god no," he says, managing to get a handle on himself so he can give me a somewhat serious look. "That would risk losing those curves of yours and then *I* would die of sadness. Plus, seeing you lose control in any way is hot as fuck for me."

"You think it's hot that I farted and came at the same time?" Forgive me if I don't believe him.

"Hell yeah," he says, catching me about the waist then hauling me on top of him. I sit back so I'm straddling him, and the fact he's still hard gets me feeling all warm again, toning down my embarrassment level. "You, my beautiful bedfellow and best friend, are what many would call 'highly strung'. You like to be in control during any given situation and don't tend to step outside your comfort zone without being pressed. So yes, seeing you lose a little of that control is a *very* attractive thing for me to witness. Shows me you're human."

Placing both of my hands over his pecs, I lean over him and smile. "Did you just call me your best friend?"

He tilts he said to the side a little and bounces a shoulder. "I did. Just don't tell Ronin I said that, he'll feel rather put out and replaced."

"You can have more than one best friend."

"You can."

"And you see me as one of yours?"

"Between you and me, I see you as top of the list. I don't hobby or fuck anyone else but you."

I don't know what it is about that sentence, but something inside me gets all warm and gooey, and I have to fight not to let my eyes fill with tears. So I lean in and kiss him instead, long, deep and slow before nudging my nose alongside his and whispering, "You're my number one best friend too."

BANKS

"Don't tell Ash, but I think I like Isla even better than I like him. And that's saying a lot," Darren says, twisting the cork out of a bottle of wine in his kitchen while I help refill the snack bowls. Theo and Isla are both in the living room, laughing at how bad we all are at Pictionary.

"I like her a lot too," I say, keeping my voice low because, as always, I'm careful not to say too much and spook her. Despite the fact we've been together for close to six months now, doing everything a normal couple would do, she still goes rigid the moment I mention anything about a future together. I've never had a serious relationship in my life, but this sure feels as close to one as a person can get without that added commitment, and even though I love every moment I spend with her, I can't help but crave for more. I don't know if it's some carnal need that goes back to our caveman roots, but there's something inside me that wants to own her completely. I want her to have my name and bear my children. The longer this relationship goes on, the more I want that. It's an urge I can't seem to shake.

"But?" Darren says, his artfully drawn brows raised as he studies my expression.

"It's nothing," I say, trying to brush it off. "Honestly, everything is great. She's great. And I'm happy."

"*But?*" he repeats, a little more forcefully this time.

"I'm fine."

Placing the cork and the bottle on the counter, Darren looks at me in a way that tells me he isn't buying a single thing I'm selling. And rightly so, these days, I'm struggling with it too. Over the last six months, I've spent every day falling harder and faster in love with Isla Wright, and I want to make her my wife.

"That's a load of shit, and you know you can't put that past me. I've known you all your life Banks Johnson. Hell, we were raised in the same house for the most part. I know you, and I also know you'd *never* bring a woman here for me to meet if she didn't mean a hell of a lot to you. So fess us, or I'm gonna march right out there and ask her."

Chewing on the inside of my lips, I run my fingers along the edge of the counter as I consider my words. While I do, a montage of every moment with Isla goes running through my head. All the laughter, the comfortable quiet, the slow walks and the long talks. Everything about her turns me on—her looks, her mind, her sense of humor, and the way she lives her life. I feel like I've genuinely found the one person in this world I align with completely, and even though we're more compatible that most couples could dream of being, she's put a major roadblock in our path. If I continue following her rules, this is it. This is as good as it gets. And I'm not sure I'm OK with that.

"I'm in love with her," I admit, causing Darren to smile cautiously.

"But that's amazing. Why are you acting like it's a bad thing?"

"Because that's not what this is supposed to be."

He frowns and moves his eyes like he's trying to work this out. "What exactly is it supposed to be?"

"At most, I suppose we're FWBs."

"Friends with benefits?" He takes a steadying breath and straightens his stance, hands crossing over his middle. "Was this her idea or yours?"

"Hers."

"And now you've caught feelings and you don't know how she's going to take it?"

"Pretty much."

"Have you discussed what happens if one of you wants more and the other doesn't?"

"Not really. It was more of an agreement that we

entered into a relationship without the option of moving it forward. She doesn't want to get married again, and because of that she also doesn't want kids."

"And you want all of that?"

"Yeah." I flash him a sardonic smile. "After the way grew up, I kind of never thought I would. Then I met her and..."

"Everything changed."

I nod.

"Same happened when I met Theo. I thought I'd be bed hopping from here to eternity, but that boy—that *man*—turned out to be the greatest thing that happened to me. But do you know what made it so wonderful?"

"You became best friends too?" Because I already know that's why I can't see myself letting go of this woman.

"Yeah. But the real reason is honesty. We've always been upfront and honest about what we want from each other."

I take in a deep, heavy breath. "So what you're saying is that I need to tell her regardless of the consequences."

Darren nods. "I know you to be a man who never backs away from a challenge, Banks. You've been a risk-taker all your life. This is just another instance where you need to risk something big to get what you want."

"That's the problem. Normally when I take a risk,

I'm willing to accept the consequences. But here, I'm not. I don't want to lose her."

"Well, cousin," he says, stepping forward and placing a hand on my arm. "Think of this this way, if you keep going the way you are right now, you're going to end up miserable and you'll lose her anyway. But that'll be long and painful instead of sharp and .fast. And I really don't want to stand by and watch you go through that."

"I suppose you're right."

Darren smiles. "You know I am." He turns his attention to the other room when laughter erupts and Theo calls out asking if we need any help. "We're fine, baby. Won't be long!" he calls back before meeting my gaze again. "Ready to go back out there?"

"Of course," I say, picking up the snack bowls and following him to where Theo and Isla are sitting on the floor, rolling about cackling.

"What on earth is happening here?" Darren asks as Isla shakes her head and points at the giant pad of paper, unable to find her voice she's laughing so hard. When we look, it's to find a crude drawing of a dick and balls.

"It's not what it looks like, I swear!" Theo says, holding up a hand as his eyes move between Darren and I.

"So you didn't create a dick pic for our female guest?"

"No!" he insists. "I was trying to draw minions. But I suck at drawing and well, without the yellow, they ended up looking like a dick."

Darren rolls his eyes as we place the snacks and wine back on the coffee table and sit back on the floor with the other. "Lucky you're pretty to look at, Theo Casey," he says, leaning over to give his man a light kiss, just as Isla gets herself under control and reaches for a pretzel on the table, munching on it while Darren and Theo exchange a few loving words along with their moment. I look at her, wishing for something exactly the same but knowing that as things are right now, I'm never going to get it.

Darren is right. It's time to take a risk. Even if it means I lose it all.

ISLA

With his mouth against mine, Banks moves inside me with long sensual, *slow* thrusts. Most of the time when we have sex, there's a certain amount of urgency, dirty words followed up by friends directions like we can't wait to finish so we can take a break and do it all again. At this time... It's different... It's like he's purposely taking his time, drawing it out in a way that makes us feel a lot more like lovemaking than pure sex. It's beautiful. But at the same time, the intensity kind of scares me.

After Banks and Darren came out of the kitchen earlier tonight, the atmosphere of the evening became somber somewhat. Before then, we'd been talking and laughing as a group, and I was feeling so glad that I agreed to a night out for a change. But then, when our wine glasses and snack bowls were refilled, we went back to the game, and despite the laughter and the jokes still being there, there was this undercurrent that made me wonder if maybe I'd done something to annoy Banks, or if maybe I'd insulting Darren somehow and he didn't like me... I tried running back through the evening as much as possible and I was at a loss as to what I'd done, which means that something else might have happened. But when I questioned Banks on the way back to my place, he assured me that everything was fine. He just had a few things on his mind.

But now, as he works through whatever those 'things' are on my body, I swear I can feel his emotions leeching in through my skin. This love making feels like sadness and longing. It feels like confusion and discontent. But most of all, it feels different. It feels like things are changing.

I'm not ready for things to change.

BANKS

With Isla's warm, slumbering body sleeping next to mine, I stare up the ceiling of her bedroom, just holding her like I might never get the chance to do it again. It's highly probable that I won't. After the way she reacted when I brought up the subject of children, I think she's been more than clear about her stance on relationships and spending her life with another person. For me, the reward for taking a risk on love feels like the ultimate gain. But for Isla, a woman who's already taken that risk and lost twice before, I realize that the risk just may not be worth it for her anymore. Which means that maybe I'm not worth it. And as much as I don't like the prospect, I think I need to walk away from that.

Glancing over to the bedside table, the numbers on the LED clock flash a green 3:16 AM. I'm obviously never going to sleep tonight, so I slowly extricate myself from around Isla's body and get out of bed, pulling on my boxers before I pad out into the kitchen in bare feet.

As I'm filling a glass with cold water from the fridge, I hear movement behind me.

"Can't sleep?" Isla asks, stopping on the other side of the island counter.

"Not really. You need a drink?" I hold out the water glass to her and she moves around the island to take it from me.

"Thank you."

"No problem," I say, grabbing another and filling it. When I replace the jug in the fridge and close it, I turn to face her, finding her sitting on top of the counter with her glass cradled between two hands.

"Want to tell me what's on your mind?" she asks, one finger tracing small circles in the condensation.

"I think it can wait until morning," I say. "You should get some sleep."

"Looks to me like we're already awake and that clock says it's morning, so..." She bounces a shoulder and takes another sip of water.

I take a deep breath then drink down the entirety of my water, stepping up to the island bench and standing beside her, placing my empty glass in the sink before gripping the edge of the marble counter and flexing my arms. Why can't I find the words?

"Hey," she says soothingly, placing a cool hand on my back. "Whatever is on your mind, you can tell me, OK? We're best friends, right?"

I smile, rocking on the soles of my feet as I gather every drop of courage I've ever had in me and force myself to meet her eyes. "I've fallen in love with you."

The serene smile she had on her face a moment ago morphs into one of surprise and confusion. "What does that mean?" she asks, her brow creasing as she sets her glass to the side.

"Exactly that. I'm in love with you, Isla. I love the way you smile, and the way you laugh. I love that you're a homebody, and I love that you're willing to learn new things. I love listening to you talk about work. And I love watching you eat food. Hell, I love watching you brush your hair and pick your nose."

"I *don't* pick my nose," she interjects, which is when I move so I'm standing between her knees, placing my hands on her thighs.

"You do a little. Everyone does a little," I say with a smirk, and she rolls her eyes.

"I am not admitting to that."

"It's OK," I say with a chuckle. "I love you, nose-picker, come-farter, puzzle-loving light of my life. And I know that at the beginning of this you said you didn't want any pressure about being something more in the future. But, Isla, it's been six months, and I can emphatically say that I don't see myself going anywhere. I want you. I need you. And damn it, I want to marry you too. I want to build a life and make a family with you. It doesn't have to be right away. I know I'm springing this on you right now, but I need you to know how I feel—what I want."

"Oh," she breathes, picking up her glass and taking a sobering sip as a battle of emotions wages a war across her face. My stomach turns sour immediately. This is exactly what I was afraid of.

"Fuck," I say, stepping away and running a hand over the top of my head. "You're still not interested, are you?"

"I didn't say that," she says, placing her glass back on the counter again. "I'm just…I'm processing."

"Sure," I say, realizing I'm sounding a little snooty because I just put myself out there and she's not immediately jumping in my arms and declaring her never-ending love for me. Logically, I knew this was the likely scenario, but damn if I didn't hope it'd turn out different anyway. "Process away."

"It's not that I don't love you, Banks. Because I do. I genuinely love everything about you…"

"But?" I say, my guts getting sicker and more twisted the longer this drags out.

"But I don't think I want to get married again. And not just to you, but to anyone."

Clasping my hands behind my head, I stretch my head back and look to the ceiling before I release my hands and blow out a breath. "OK. So a couple of assholes before me ruined my chance with you, and that means no marriage, no kids, and that's that?"

"I don't know what to say to that. I'm sorry, Banks," she says, emotion shaking in her voice. "I'm just trying to be honest about how I feel."

"I know. And I appreciate it. I'm just trying to do the same here."

"I know. And I appreciate it too. But I can't change how I feel."

"Yeah," I say, scrubbing a hand over my face. "Me either."

"Banks," she says, as I walk back to the bedroom with my hands on my hips. "I'm so sorry."

"Me too," I say, pulling on my jeans and grabbing my T-shirt too.

"You're leaving?"

"Yeah." I pull the tee over my head and pick up my shoes. "And I know this looks like I'm throwing a tantrum because I'm not getting my way—and maybe I am—but yeah, I'm leaving."

"I really wish you wouldn't. We're so great together. We...just work, don't we? Am I wrong there?"

"Yeah, we work, Isla. We're fucking fantastic together. You tick every fucking box along with a bunch I didn't even know I had, but then there's these optional extra boxes that I really fucking want, but you've already ticked those boxes in your past, and you didn't like the way it was served so you just don't fucking want it anymore. But I do. I want to try. I don't want to stay just as we are, then be sitting there doing puzzles together when we're eighty, looking back and regretting that we never took the plunge together. Because I want to do that with you. I fucking want all of that relationship stuff. And I'm not gonna keep doing this, hoping you'll change your mind, or worse, guilting you into doing something you don't want just to keep my happy. So, for your sake, and for mine"—I finish tying my laces and stand from the edge of the bed—"I think it's best if I go back to my place, and you find some other guy to have a no relationship with. Turns out, I'm not as capable at it as I thought I would be."

"Banks!" she cries, her hand wrapping around my arm as I pass her to walk out the door. "Please don't leave like this."

"I have to, Isla," I whisper, leaning my forehead against hers. "I can't change the way I feel, and neither can you. I'm sorry."

"Me too," she gasps, hiccupping when I press a soft kiss against her lips and then her forehead, before I finally let her go and head out of her apartment, her soft sobbing echoing behind as my heart turns heavy in my chest. I just blew it big time. *Fuck*.

ISLA

"What the actual fuck?" Karen says, her mouth dropping open the moment she enters my office on Monday morning. For once I beat her in. After a weekend spent crying and wallowing in my own self pity, I just had to get out of my apartment and do something productive. "What happened to your face?"

"Banks and I broke up," I inform her, the tone in my voice gone because I think I might have forgotten how to feel now. The whole point of Banks's and my arrangement was to *avoid* situations like this. But it just goes to show I'm incapable of having any sort of adult relationship without it turning into a shambles.

"Oh no," she coos, immediately closing and locking the door before sliding into the chair in front of my desk and placing a hand on my arm. "What happened."

I shake my head, my stupid tears burning against the back of my eyes when I was sure I'd run out of the darn things. "He wants more. I told him I can't give it to him. So he left."

"Oh shit, sweetie. I know how much you liked him too. I'm so sorry."

"I didn't just like him, Karen. I loved him. He was everything I ever wanted—my friend, my lover, my confidant, my rock. We were so good together, and I honestly thought we were on the same page. But then…"

"He changed the rules," she finishes for me, passing over the box of tissues so I can dab at my already swollen eyes. I couldn't even wear my contacts today because they were so sore, so I push my glasses to the top of my head and dab at my eyes to stem the flow.

"I should have seen this coming," I say once I've calmed down. "He asked me about kids a few months ago, and I explained that I wasn't willing to bring a child into this world when I can't guarantee stability, and I thought he was OK with that. He said he understood."

"Does he want kids?"

"Yeah. He said he wants it all—the wedding, the kids, the happy ever after."

She smiles softly. "And what do you want?"

I look up and meet her green eyes. "I want to not feel like this," I say, a fresh bout of tears flowing down my cheeks. "It's not that I don't want kids myself—I do. I just don't want to mess them up the way every kid in my family is messed up. Taking marriage off the table in the beginning was supposed to be the thing that stopped things from ending like this. But it seems I'm doomed to repeat the same cycle, over and over. I just…I can't do this again. I'm not equipped to keep getting my heart broken."

"Oh honey." She places her hand on mine and gives it a squeeze. "It's not marriage that's the enemy here. From what I know and saw of your past relationships, it was the men being narcistic cunts that caused your unhappiness. I don't think Banks is like that."

"So what are you saying? That I should backflip on everything I've said and give into the guy? I thought you hated the idea of marriage."

"I do," she says, taking a steady breath as she searches my eyes and pleads for understanding. "And I'm not telling you to backflip, but I am going to point out that you have been married before. So that means you believed in it once – twice, even —so I guess what I'm saying is that you just have to have a good look at this situation and do what's right for you. Are you against marriage because it failed? Or do you hate it deep down to your core? Because I kind of get the sense that you don't hate marriage, you hate having your heart broken."

I nod as I dab my tissue at my eye. "You're right. I do."

"If you love Banks the way you say you do, then maybe he's worth taking the risk of trying again for? Maybe, since you've already built a relationship on honesty, friendship and trust, you'll have a marriage like that too. And I'm not saying that you have to run out and marry the guy right away then start popping out his children, but maybe…just maybe…it's worth reconsidering."

"If Andy came to you and said he wanted to get married and start a family, would you give yourself the same advice?"

Pressing her lips together, she laces her hands in her lap and sits back against her chair with a sigh. "I know. I sound like a hypocrite. But Andy and I have a different set of values than most—and we will have kids one day, they just won't be born in wedlock. But to answer your question, if he came to me and explained that it was a relationship-ending decision for him to get married, then yes, I would consider it. Sometimes little pieces of paper and gold bands are important to people, and in the grand scheme of things, it wouldn't change *how I* love him, but if it makes him feel more complete, I'm OK with that. But I wouldn't change my name," she says, smiling as she pushes up from the chair. "That's mine. I guess what I'm saying here is to just follow your heart, Isla. Love is about compromise, it's about giving a little to get something really amazing in return, and from how happy you've been this past six months with Banks... gosh I'd hate to see you give that up because of a couple of turd burgers who treated you badly. You deserve your happy ever after—marriage, no marriage, kids, no kids. Whatever it is *your* heart wants, go out there and make it happen."

"Gosh. You've made all the mush in my head even mushier."

"I know. But you're gonna be OK. And I'll still be here no matter what you decide." I nod, blowing out a heavy breath as she exits my office, leaving me on my own with a hell of a lot to think about, because at the end of the day, I don't really know what I want anymore. Well...besides Banks, of course. But the question is, can I want what Banks wants?

I have a lot of soul searching to do.

BANKS

"You look like shit." I step back as Ronan pushes his way into my apartment and takes a slow look around. "When was the last time you cracked a window in here?" He lifts the lid of an empty pizza box then dusts off his hands. "Better yet, when was the last time you went outside? Took a shower? Shaved?"

"I've showered," I grumble, picking up the pizza box and as many empty beer bottles as I can manage. Ronan scoops up the rest of the mess and follows me into the kitchen, tossing it into the trash before he lets out a steady breath.

"Talk to me, man. This isn't you."

"Yeah. Well, it is now." I move back into the living room and drop my weight onto the couch, putting my feet up on the coffee table.

Ronan takes the seat next to me. "You know, in all the years I've known you, I've never seen you torn up over a single girl. What was it that is different about this one?"

I shrug as I fold my arms across my chest. "She got me. I could be myself around her."

"Could she be herself around you?"

"Yeah. It was the whole point of us being together. We wanted someone who liked similar things and who it *felt* good to be with. We were just so fucking compatible, and I've never had that with anyone in my life before. But she didn't want any strings and I...well, I did."

"And now it's over. Just like that?"

I shrug again. "I'm not sure how it's supposed to keep going when we both want different things."

"What do you mean you both want different things, man? When you started dating Isla, you told me she's twice divorced and really nervous about repeating the mistakes of her past, right?"

"Right."

"And then you said that you were going to *prove* to her that you weren't anything like those other guys. You said you were gonna stick it out, no matter how hard she pushed because you *knew* you two were made for each other."

"Yeah, but—"

"But what, Banks? What's fucking changed?"

"I told her I want more, and she said she didn't."

"Forever?"

"Jesus, Ronan! I don't fucking know. Maybe after six months, she's just realized that I'm not the guy for her."

"Bull-fucking-shit. I think you just threw a bomb at her feet and when she didn't give you what you wanted, you high tailed it out of there."

"Fuck off. I was just honest about how I feel."

"As was she. Right from the start, right? She said she didn't want to get married again. And when you brought up kids, she didn't say she didn't want them—she just said she didn't want them unless she was sure she was in a stable relationship. One where her partner doesn't throw a fucking tantrum and leave her when he doesn't get his way."

"That's not fair. I'm allowed to want what I want."

"Yeah, you are. And I love you, man. You're the closest thing to a brother I've ever had. But this isn't you. You're not the kind of guy who walks away. I mean, imagine you did get married and then later on you found out she *couldn't* have kids—would you leave her then?"

My mouth drops open, but my gut twists up tight. I really don't want to hear this. But damn, he's right. "No," I say, shaking my head. "I would never."

He places a hand on my shoulder and gives it a

squeeze. "So why are you giving up now? You love her, right?"

"Of course."

"So what would you rather do? Go and find some other girl to marry and have kids with? Or be happy and in love, taking a risk with Isla? She might change her mind, but she might not. Either way, do you really want to give what you have with her up?"

Looking across the room to the crate I put all our cross-stitch stuff in, I think back over the many hours we've spent together just being...us. And when I think of a future without that, it's bleak as fuck. I want her back. However she comes, whatever the future holds, one thing is absolutely certain. She and I belong to each other.

"I want to spend my life with Isla."

He claps me on the back. "Then you gotta go out there and get her, brother. Do the grand gesture."

"Such as?"

"Tell me the one thing you can get her that she can't get herself?"

"Fuck. There isn't a lot she wants. Despite her name and her money, she likes simplicity. What she cares most about is fairness and being an agent of change when her and her cousins take over Wright Media. Not that any of those old guys seem willing to step down any time soon."

Ronan grins as he sits forward and pulls his cell from his back pocket. "I have an idea."

"What kind of idea?"

"Well, what are you and I both really good at?"

"Knowing the right business to invest in and which ones to steer clear of."

"Exactly. We've made a lot of people a lot of money."

"I have no idea how that's supposed to help anything here. I'm not looking to invest."

"No. But we know lots of people who invest in everything from bank bonds to bitcoin. Between us, I reckon know every broker, banker or financer on Wall St. That means, that with our powers combined—"

"Holy fuck, Ronan," I say, his plan dawning on me and straightening my spine as energy floods my veins for the first time since I walked out of Isla's apartment. "You're brilliant."

He laughs while he fires off a bunch of messages. "It's why they pay me the big bucks, my friend. You want power? I can find a way to get it for you."

And as we work through our combined contacts in an effort to formulate our plan, I wonder if it's going to be enough to show Isla how much she means to me. I hate to admit it, but blindsiding her the way I did then storming off was childish. I let my pride get in the way of the facts that were laid out before me. I'm in love with Isla. And she's in love with me. At our very core, she and I want the same things, but what Isla really needs is someone to standby and support her because no one else before me has. Everything else? Well, we'll work it out eventually. But one thing is certain, I can't walk away from her. I never should have, and I'm going to bend over backwards and accomplish something huge for her to prove to her that I'll never turn my back again.

ISLA

"Does anyone even know who called this meeting? Or what it's about?" my Uncle Bruce asks, frowning at his watch as he sits in his big chair at the head of the boardroom table, Wright Media's logo proudly displayed on the wall behind him, framing him like it's the halo of power.

To his left is my father, Paul, and to his right is my other uncle, Graham. They nod, backing Bruce up as they look across the table to my cousins and me.

"I didn't have anything to do with this," one says, while the other lifts his hands and adds that it wasn't him either.

All eyes fall on me. "Well, it definitely wasn't *me*," I shoot back with a frown. "We're not the only people in this world with the power to call a shareholder's meeting."

"We're the only people with enough collective power to vote on anything," my father points out. "Whoever called this meeting had better have a good explanation or I'll be billing them for all of our time."

I press my lips together, deciding it's not worth entering into any further debate until we know exactly why we're all here. Bruce taps his fingers on the table obnoxiously, and when the door finally opens, I almost want to kiss whoever it is just for making that impatient grumbling stop.

But then, I turn to see who it is, and I don't just want to kiss him. After a huge amount of thought and soul searching, I think I might want to marry him—if he'll still have me, of course. Third time's the charm, right?

"Banks?" I say on a gasp, shooting to my feet as he steps through wearing one of his tailored suits and a stony expression.

"You know this man?" my father asks, to which I nod and slowly lower myself back into my seat, the absence of any sort of warmth in Banks's eyes making the contents of my stomach sour. He's not here for me. And after refusing to consider his proposal when we last saw each other, maybe I deserve that. Maybe I deserve whatever's coming here. *I should have said yes. I should have at least said I'd think about it.* But instead, I watched him walk out of my apartment and my life. I have so much regret now.

"Good morning, all," Banks says, business in his tone as he ushers in his friend Ronan. "We're still waiting on a couple of people, but we have their permission to get this ball rolling in the meantime."

"Exactly what is this about? Who are you jokers?" Bruce bellows, his jowly cheeks shaking along with his frustration.

"We," Ronan starts as he and Banks take a seat, "are representative of the bulk percentage of your shareholders. And we come with a proposition for you."

"You think you own the bulk of Wright Media's shares?" Uncle Graham scoffs. "That's impossible. The family owns control."

"You're right," Banks says. "Each member of the Wright family has a certain amount of shares in their portfolio, giving the family that magical fifty-one percent to swing any motion to challenge leadership."

Uncle Bruce starts chuckling, my father and Graham joining in before Bruce abruptly slaps the table. "You've got rocks in your head if that's what you think is happening today."

"Not rocks," Ronan says, opening a folder in front of him and taking out a sheet of paper. "A different number." He pushes the sheet of paper across the table, and the older generation snatches it up before muttering things about impossibilities.

"So," Banks starts, addressing the three brothers clearly, "in a vote to replace the current leadership with the next in line, Isla Wright, Kenyon Wright and Darius Wright, all we'd need is one percent more." Banks's eyes swing to me, warming just a touch before they move onto my cousins. "The swing vote will fall to you three."

Warmth blooms in my chest as Banks finds my eyes again and lets that cool façade of his slip just enough for me to read his intentions. And it really is all about me.

Without being asked, without knowing how I'd respond, and without any guarantee this Hail Mary of his will pay off, he's stormed the castle of Wright Media to fight off the dragons so his Rapunzel can take her rightful place in this world—at the head of Wright Media. This beautiful man is giving me the one thing I've always wanted and never been able to get for myself. The chance to make a difference. And if I hadn't decided I wanted to marry him before, I certainly do now. Hell, I might even give him babies after this one too. He's truly proving his staying power and the lengths he'll go to to fight for me.

"*Thank you,*" I mouth to him, tears catching in my eyes as his turn tender before he nods then turns back to Ronan.

"Fifty percent!" Bruce yells, slamming the piece of paper on the table. "How on earth could you even manage that? It's impossible."

"That's a question I can answer for you, father," a

voice from the doorway says, causing us all to turn our attention to Tanner Wright, Bruce's only son and original heir to the company throne. He's also been marred as public enemy number one after dragging his father through the courts to make him honor his commitments to Tanner's disabled sister, Camille. It was a PR nightmare and saw our share price plummet. I did *not* enjoy work while that storm was brewing, but I still understand why Tanner did it.

"You don't own enough shares to do this," his father responds.

"I didn't," he says, grinning like the cat who got the cream. "But as Camille's court-appointed guardian, I control her shares, and Ash, well, he very kindly sold me his. So now I do."

"I vote with Tanner!" Kenyon yells, shooting his hand in the air like he's in grade school.

"Me too," Darius joins in, meaning I have a massive smile on my face as I nod and look back to Banks.

"Me too," I say, wishing I could reach him from where I'm sitting to at least hold his hand. As it is, all I can think about is touching his skin again, kissing him and making never-ending love to him. He's just given me the most wonderful gift, and I don't think I can ever repay him. But I'm sure going to try.

"The 'I's have it," Ronan says, standing up as he closes his folder and grins. "Let the minutes reflect that Isla Wright, Kenyon Wright and Darius Wright are the new heads of Wright Media effective immediately."

"You...You can't...You can't do this!" Bruce bellows, his head shaking as he looks to his brothers who just sit in stunned silence. I don't think I've ever seen my father or my uncles look dumbstruck before. But now, looking at all three of them sitting there with their mouths open and their eyes bugging out, I realize that no one has ever kept them down before either. They've lived so long with their power that they just couldn't let it go.

"We have, and we did. Best of luck, and we'll see you at the next shareholders' meeting," Banks says, standing with Ronan and heading out with Tanner, leaving us all in the boardroom with our stunned parents.

"You've betrayed us," Graham says, completely bewildered.

"Technically, father," Darius says as he rises from his seat. "You three have been betraying us all along by refusing to retire and refusing to make changes that would actually see this company grow instead of turning into the dinosaur of print it's becoming. Now that we're in charge, we'll be able to start diversifying like we always wanted to do, and you can sit back and watch your dividends roll in while you enjoy the sweet life of retirement. You're welcome."

Before any of them can formulate a response,

Darius, Kenyon and I file out of the boardroom, noting that we need to sit down together and prepare for what's next. I couldn't agree more, but right now, there's something else I need to do that's far more important than anything to do with this company. I have to find Banks.

Excusing myself, I head straight for the elevator bay, hitting the button rapid fire until a car arrives and I jump inside, banging at the lobby button like it'll make this thing go any faster.

"Come on, come on." My heart is beating wildly and the only thing I'm concerned about right now is finding Banks and telling him I was wrong. There's a reason he and I found each other, and I'd have rocks in my head if I thought keeping us from building a future together would somehow protect my heart. Because it didn't. I fell in love with him body, mind and soul, and every day without him is just a waste. And I don't want to waste time anymore.

The moment the door pings open, I shoot out into the lobby, looking everywhere for the top of Banks's head in the crowd. He should be easy to spot since he's in a group of three giant men, but when I can't find him, I make a dash for the exit, shooting out onto the sidewalk and looking in both directions.

"Banks!" I call out, not because I see him, but in the hope he'll hear me and stop moving. But as I swivel my head left to right and find nothing, I all but give up.

That's when I hear the unmistakable rattle of lots of little pieces inside a cardboard box. *Banks.*

With a happy gasp in my chest, I spin around and find Banks standing against my building with a puzzle in his hand and a smile on his face. "I thought we could go somewhere and puzzle this out."

Tears heat my eyes as my feet carry me at top speed, slamming my body into his chest as my arms wrap around his neck. "I missed you so much," I cry, clinging to him and crying into his neck. "I'm so sorry I chased you away."

"I'm sorry I left," he murmurs near my ear, his hands moving to cup either side of my head as he pulls us apart slightly so he can look me in the eye. "I'm sorry I tried to change the rules. I'm sorry I considered doing a single thing that could make you not be in my life anymore. I love you, Isla, and I want to be with you. I don't care how. I just want you, and I want to see you happy. I hope what we did up there in that boardroom goes some of the way to show you how serious I am."

With tears streaming out of my eyes now, I nod, taking a deep breath to steady my voice so I can speak. "I want to get married," I blurt, loving the way his eyes pop and his smile widens as the words leave my life.

"Are you kidding me?"

"No. I've been thinking long and hard about it, and I never had what we have before. I was stupid and reckless before, getting married for all the wrong reasons, but with you, Banks, all those reasons are right. You're my best friend. You're my heart. And you're my soul too. So, if there's anyone in this world worth risking my heart on, it's you. Because you own it anyway. From the day you marked my thigh with your name, I belonged to you. And I really hope you still want to belong to me."

"Abso-fucking-lutely," he says, bringing his mouth to mine and kissing me so long and hard that I never want to let him go. And I won't, because while I was scared of what might come before, I'm not anymore. Banks has just done the impossible, he's forced my uncles to retire, and he's taught this skeptic that true love and happily ever afters really do exist. He and I are living proof of that, and together, we can do anything.

EPILOGUE - BANKS

Twelve months later...

"Are you guys seriously planning on driving all the way to Atlanta?" Ronan says as I hand him the keys to the bar so he can watch over it for me while we're gone. "That's a solid thirteen hours on the road."

"Which is why we're taking our time, sight seeing and checking in a hotel along the way. Isla is too pregnant to fly, so this is better than her going into labor at high altitude."

"Dude, all you're doing is risking her giving birth on the side of the road."

"She's thirty-four weeks. We're gonna be fine." It's at that moment my darling fiancée hits the horn to hurry me along. "I should get going," I add with a smile. "Hormones make her impatient."

Ronan laughs as he leans around me and waves to Isla. "I'll take good care of the bar for you. Drive safe. Keep my favorite girl happy." I'm one of the lucky ones whose best guy friend gets along with his partner like a house on fire. Despite Isla's protestations that she prefers to be home more than she likes socializing, she sure is good at it. I don't have a single friend or family member she hasn't won over with her easy smile and can-do attitude. My parents think she's amazing, and I'm sure that if my gran was still with us, she'd love her too.

"Will do. And thanks. I appreciate it."

"Any time. Enjoy the wedding."

Yes, a wedding. But, no, it's not my and Isla's wedding. That's going to come in the near future—some time after the twins are born so they can be little flower girls for us. It's going to be great. Just like Isla's and my relationship has been from the get go.

Sure, we kind of started things a little backward, but once we got to know each other and realized the both of us would be willing to move heaven and earth for the other, there was nothing left standing in our way.

These days, I'm still running the bar, but I also have a small role to play in Ronan's new company that he started after his promotion didn't pan out the way he expected. He decided that if he wanted to be the king of Wall St, he'd have to handpick the people he works with and build a business from scratch. I'm more of a silent partner than a fully-fledged and active partner, but for a control freak like Ronan, it works well. I help him out when he needs it, and in turn, he's always willing to help me. I think the free vodka might have a lot to do with it, though.

Work wise for Isla, everything has been going great as well, she got to become the contributing member of Wright Media that she always wanted to be. And when she's not working, she loves spending time on her new hobby—painting pictures and turning them into puzzles.

When we moved in together a couple of months after reuniting, I insisted we have a room dedicated to hobbies. It's in there that we spend the vast majority of our downtime, enjoying each other's company while working on projects that help reinvigorate our minds so we can go out there and face the hustle bustle of the world again come Monday morning.

I wouldn't say we're both total introverts, but we definitely ride the line of needing plenty of time to recharge in the quiet of our home in between our busy work and social life. So with that in mind, taking a couple of days out between now and her brother, Ash's wedding in Atlanta is just the getaway the both of us need leading up to us becoming busy parents. It's something we're both really looking forward to, but since it's the first time for us both, we know we're going to be in for a learning experience. Two babies at once is not going to be easy.

"You need to pee before we leave, gorgeous?" I ask when I climb back into the car and lean across the console to press a kiss against her sweet lips.

"I'm fine. But we both know that could change in the next fifteen minutes, so I've plotted our route with every gas station and fast-food outlet marked just in case. I am *not* going to be squatting by the side of the street. I'll get stuck down there like that weird witch lady in Dark Crystal who can remove her eye." She does an impression of Magra grunting and groaning and I immediately imagine the scene from the movie.

"Oh, honey, those are the noises you make whenever you get up off the couch," I tease, lacing my fingers with hers once we've settled into the stream of traffic to start our journey.

She gasps in mock horror. "You are so mean."

"I happen to love the sound of you groaning. Getting off the couch or otherwise." I lift her hand and press a kiss to her knuckles.

"You are too smooth, Mr. Banks," she teases in return. "Keep that up, and when we get to that hotel tonight, I'll be the one to make *you* moan and groan."

"Can't wait," I say, waggling my eyebrows and looking forward to every bit of this trip we've planned together. Better yet, I can't wait for the rest of this life we've planned together.

ISLA

"Um... Banks?" I wake to the warm gush of something flowing between my legs, unable to stop it, I realize it's my water. The damn thing just broke.

"Mmm?" His sleepy arm slides over my well-rounded belly. "Everything OK?"

"My water just broke."

"What?" He sits up ramrod straight and flicks the light on, jumping out of bed and babbling stuff about it being too soon, and the birth plan, and how are we supposed to get back to our OBGYN in time when the babies could come at any moment. "This is too soon!"

"I know," I say, laughing despite the tension of the moment because my beautiful fiancé is having a bit of a meltdown and one of us needs to be calm. "You're going to have to drive me to the nearest hospital."

"OK. I can do that," he says, pulling on his clothes and becoming a whirlwind packing machine.

I get up and he's straight at my side, helping me get my clothes and shoes on. Then he just stops and looks at me with wide eyes.

"The babies are gonna be OK, right?"

Reaching out, I touch his face and press my lips to his in a soft kiss. "I think they're gonna be great. If they're anything like you and me, they're just too impatient to keep on waiting for the things they want."

"I like that idea," he says, nodding as he looks around to make sure we have everything. "Let's go. Do you want me to carry you? Are you in pain?"

"No pain. Just a little crampy. But I'm OK. Nervous, but OK."

He stops as he pulls open the room door and looks back at me. "I'm nervous too. We're about to be parents, Isla. Fucking parents."

"I know," I whisper, leaning up against his broad chest as I gaze up at him lovingly. "And we're going to be great at it."

With a quick kiss and a steadying breath, we bustle out of the room and down to the car, heading straight for the nearest hospital where we spend several hours monitoring the babies and me before they decide they've had enough of waiting and make their way into the world less than two minutes apart.

"Seems we missed the wedding," Banks says as we cradle the girls in our arms after the arduous task of giving birth to them and cleaning up after is complete, and we're alone in our room. Despite them being early, they're strong and more than ready to be part of this world. We've been asked to stay in the hospital for a couple of days to monitor them, but so far, so good. Our girls, Kylie and Kaylie, just couldn't wait to meet us.

"I think Ash and Tahlia will understand," I whisper, marveling at the dark wispy curls on our girls' heads and the little snuffly noises they make as we huddle together and just cuddle up as a family for the first time.

"Do you want to call them and let them know why we didn't show?"

"Just tell them we ended up taking a detour and got waylaid. That way, they get to keep their day and the wedding is all about them."

"You sure?"

"Yeah. Ash will understand that there's no way I'd miss his wedding if I couldn't help it. And you know they'll all rush out here the moment they find out. So give them their special night, and we'll make it up to them when we tell them tomorrow they got nieces as a wedding gift."

"OK, I'm texting from your phone. Saying that we went to the wrong place, but we promise we'll make it up to them later."

Leaning into his shoulder, I smile, because that's exactly how we started—by ending up in the wrong place. And even though I didn't think I would ever be ready for a serious relationship again, that wrong place ended up being the right time for both of us. Just like this was the right time for the twins. And like their parents, they didn't come into this world following the rules. I'd like to think they followed their little hearts, just like Banks and I have been in our journey to each other. Sure, we haven't done much of anything the 'right' or traditional way. But we've done it in a way that has made us happy. And because of that, I know deep in my heart that we share a love that will last a lifetime. With a man like Banks on my side, anything feels possible.

THE END...*ISH*

Want some more fun-loving action in the Wrong, Wright world? Wall St Jerk featuring Ronan is up next.

Click 'follow' on Amazon when the rating window pops up on your device so the kindle app will notify you of new releases.

ALSO BY MEGAN WADE

Novels

Standalone

Mine for the Holidays

Wrong/Wright Series

Wrong Car, Wright Guy

Wrong Room, Wright Girl

Wrong Place, Wright Time

Novellas

Cocktails & Curves Series

Swipe for a Cosmo

Old Fashioned Sweetie

Dark & Stormy Darlin'

Made by Manhattan

Happy Curves Series

Sheets & Giggles

Quilts & Chuckles

Sweet Curves Series

Marshmallow

Pumpkin

Pop

Sugarplum

Cookie

Sucker

Taffy

Toffee Apple

Peaches & Cream

Cupcake

Cheesecake

Wedded Curves Series

Whoa! I married a Mountain Man!

Whoa! I married a Billionaire!

Whoa! I married the Pitcher!

Whoa! I Married a Rock Star!

Whoa! I Married a Biker!

Sugar Curves

Sugar Honey Ice Tea

Yikes on a Cracker

What the Hell-o Kitty-Kat

Horse's Ask

Holy Cannoli

Hells Bells & Taco Shells

Holy Frozen Snowcones

Son of a Nutcracker

Collaborations

Cillian (The Kelly Brothers)

The Not So Silent Night (Santa's Coming)

Unexpected Sweetheart (Sweetheart, Colorado)

Sweet Ride (Men of Valor)

Drink it Down (Getting Lucky)

518 Hope Ave (Cherry Falls)

Deep, Deep Donuts (Lovers Lake)

GET IN TOUCH WITH MEGAN WADE

Megan Wade is a simple girl who believes in love at first sight and soulmates. She's obsessed with happy endings and Hallmark is her favorite brand of everything. Each Megan Wade story carries her 'Sugar Promise' of Over the Top Romance, Alpha Heroes, Curvy Heroines, Low Drama, High Heat and a Guaranteed Happily Ever After. What could be better than that?

email: contact@meganwadebooks.com

Newsletter: Get a copy of Rowdy Prince FREE when you sign up and confirm: https://www.subscribepage.com/meganwade_freebie

Amazon follow: click 'follow' on Amazon when the

rating window pops up on your device so the kindle app will notify you of new releases.

Facebook: https://www.facebook.com/meganwadeauthor/

Sweeties group: https://www.facebook.com/groups/959211654464973

Instagram: https://www.instagram.com/meganwadewrites/

Made in United States
North Haven, CT
18 March 2024

50122250R00104